THE ABSENT THERAPIST

Will Eaves is the author of three novels (most recently, *This Is Paradise*, Picador, 2012) and a collection of poetry (*Sound Houses*, Carcanet, 2011). He was Arts Editor of the *Times Literary Supplement* from 1995 to 2011, and now teaches at the University of Warwick.

'The pieces in *The Absent Therapist* often resound with truth, whether the overheard voice is that of a plumber offering to redo another tradesman's botched job, a Londoner describing spanking in a gay club, or a businessman losing his listener's interest by spouting jargon about bridge documents, tech guys and new gen stuff. The fragments range across continents – America, Africa, Australia – as well as classes, and many of them are clearly situated . . . Others are decontextualised, and often these are the most arresting, either for their meditative quality or through a poetic suggestiveness which reminds us that Eaves is a poet as well as a writer of prose fiction.'
    – *Times Literary Supplement*

'*The Absent Therapist* is a slim book with no single plot, yet the author's decision to call it a novel seems justified: these confluent streams of consciousness amount to a narrative in prose where every comma is vital for the flow to run as it does . . . The voices you hear give the impression of having been selected with some degree of randomness – "a story worth telling", the author says, can be found where you least expect it – but their arrangement is precise down to the last dropped aitch.'
    – Anna Aslanyan, *3:AM*

also by Will Eaves

WILL EAVES

The Absent Therapist

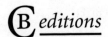

CB editions

ACKNOWLEDGEMENTS

The author would like to thank the editors of *The Warwick Review*, *Yale Review* and the *Picador Book of 40*, in whose pages earlier versions of 'The Absent Therapist', 'Where Do You Get Your Tired Ears From?' and 'We Are Prey' first appeared.

Printed in England by Blissetts, London W3 8DH

ISBN 978–1–909585–00–3

There are, it may be, so many kinds of voices in the world, and none of them is without signification.

– 1 Corinthians 14:10

———

I   The Absent Therapist

I had a last look round for the key and then took it to Fortress, who were closed, of course. After that I decided to have a go with my penknife and jemmied it open in about ten seconds. And, as I suspected, it contained my birth certificate but not the photos I'd been kidding myself I hadn't lost. On the other hand, I did find my Whippet Club Centenary badge (1899–1999) and the programme from Hemel Hempstead, where Whisper won the Burger Bar stakes at 8.47 p.m. Whisper's full name was Whispering Softly and, oh, she was a headstrong animal, never came when you called, which I didn't all that much. You couldn't go round shouting WHISPER! WHISPER!, could you? The comments said, 'EP Ran on Well', EP for 'Early Pace'. She was up against Marlow Dusty, Jimmy the Hoover, Little Minnie, Louisiana Venture, and Rye. She'd had just that one race before, a four-dog trial with the early pace, and Dad was so pleased when she won. Whisper was more his dog than mine. I only bred a single litter, but I got Bacardi Breeze out of it and she was a runner-up in the East Anglia Whippet Coursing Club Trials in 2002. That earned her a rosette and a two-line write-up in *Dog World*, which also went in the box. Bacardi Breeze wasn't her real name and I've been worrying over and over about what it was. Dad would remember, that's for sure.

It might have been Misty. Maybe it was. Misty bolted from the house one morning and came back an hour later with a bow-tie round her neck. Where she got it from we never knew. She kept that tie on for months.

———

He wrote back without giving his number. He said he had to be discreet as he was well known in the Perth area, but if I could place an ad in the *Voice* for a green lounge suite with my number attached he would ring it, the idea being that no one in their right minds would want a green lounge suite so the only person answering would be him. It did seem a little complicated, even to my innocent mind, but then I thought, perhaps he's famous? Perhaps it's Jason Donovan! And I began to get excited. So I placed the ad and of course it turned out that several boho couples who were refurbishing apartments in Mount Lawley felt that a green lounge suite would be just the ticket, and I had to disappoint them all. 'I'm sorry. It's just gone.' Some of them were suspicious. How come I'd sold it so quickly? How many other people in Perth wanted a green lounge suite? Then Peter rang and said 'You've been on the phone a while' and I said, 'What is it you do, anyway?' He said, 'I'll tell you when we meet', and we arranged, finally, to meet at the station café. He would be wearing a suit and tie and reading the *Voice*. How would he recognise me? I, too, would be in a suit. 'What colour?' he asked, and I said 'green', thinking he'd appreciate the joke, and he put the phone down.

———

Owen has the kind of lack of self-awareness that makes you think it must be a dare, him seeing what he can get away with before someone says, 'Are you, or have you recently gone, totally mad?' I like him, but he needs his whole mental world completely realigned. He was telling the office the other day – well, speaking on the phone, but shouting, shouting, *shouting* with the door open so we could all hear – how French people mistake him for a native because of his amazing accent. Trying to make it sound as if he was being modest, you know. 'Oh, I'm not all that fluent. I mean, I get *by* in conversation perfectly well. But the accent fools people because it's really very authentic-sounding, so I'm told. People think I must be French, you see.' And I thought, really? Who are these people, Owen? The relatives of Helen Keller?

———

I did know the Prince quite well, yes. Well, no, not *that* well. He went out with my friend Rebecca for a while and I think she found it a struggle. She used to come to my room with a bag over her head to avoid the paparazzi. But I was in plays and he was interested in the theatre, and our paths crossed. I remember bumping into him in Sainsbury's, during the Easter vacation. I was up trying to write a dissertation on Webster, and suddenly there we were, he and I, and his bodyguard – Jim – looking grim in front of the digestives. I said to Prince Edward, 'What are you still doing here?', and he said he'd stayed on to write his dissertation as well. 'I can't really do it at home, you know,' he said. 'You know how it is.' And

I didn't know what to say to that. I mean, I thought of my house, in Harlow, with the small sitting room and my parents and grandmother and my three brothers and my sister, and the box room I still slept in, and the telly on, and no books, and I couldn't say anything. I thought, what? Can't you decide which home to write in? I had an audition two years later, for *Aspects of Love*, when he was 'setting up' his company, and Heaven knows what kind of struggle that must have been, and I said 'hi' from the stage, and he blanked me. *You know how it is.*

―――――

Catherine was involved in a car accident last week. Hyde Park Corner, five lanes of traffic. She wasn't in the accident itself. She was a few cars back, but she got out and ran to help, and sat there in the road, holding this lady with massive head injuries, calling for an ambulance. The woman bled to death in her arms. The ambulance and the police arrived and a man said to her, 'Is there someone at home, love?' Nobody offered her a lift or ordered a taxi. And she said she'd be fine – avoiding the question, she said – and she went back to her flat. Her mac and her clothes, her shoes and her hands completely covered with the woman's blood. She was in shock when she rang me and thank God I wasn't at the ruddy PTA. Thank God I was at home when Cathy rang.

―――――

Mystery shoppers call around four. They're supposed to be undetectable. You're supposed to think they're legitimate enquiries, but they're always obviously fake, which shows how much management know about what we do, what it's like to field calls all day, if they think their efforts are remotely plausible. That said, most of the real people who *do* ring us are certifiable, and not as dentists, so perhaps it makes no odds. I hadn't had a mystery shopper for some weeks and then the woman with asthma who's just been promoted rings me and says, 'Good morning, I'd like to be a specialist.' And I say, 'But you work in HR.' To which she replies: 'Can you tell me how I'd go about becoming a specialist?' So I ask her whether or not she has any relevant specialist qualifications and she says no. She's beginning to pant. 'Can I still, *hup*, be a specialist?' In my monthly review my manager said that 'clearly not' was a good and helpful answer. The only thing I might have considered adding was, 'Is there anything else I can help you with today?'

———

And Lionel was brought up by a tyrannous Uncle, who ended up in a locked ward, so in many ways thank goodness for the Second World War which saved Lionel from his, shall we say, less than promising domestic circumstances. Then after the war he became a GP and taught himself to plumb in his spare time. He fitted the appliances here. Did you smell any gas in the night? I got a whiff when I was passing through to the toilet. It's a kerosene gas fridge and it's burning yellow now. I've been trying to clean the ceramic lighter, which is – can you see? – a very delicate little mechanism, very delicate indeed. It might be chipped, I think. But it's part of the experience. This is a *shack*, after all, not a holiday home. The tap-dancing mice are an integral part of it, too. They belong here. If you can just help me push the fridge back, use your hip, *that's* it, there we go. So there's no gap between it and the wall. Then nothing can fall down. Rodents, small children. The floor? What about it? Ah no, there we must agree to differ. The state of the floor is not in fact as alarming as it might seem. What appear to be myriad droppings could well be insect cocoons, larval casings or desiccated moths, so let's not be *too* liberal *too* quickly with the *Talon*. A little poison goes a long way, as my widowed aunt used to say. It's certainly not as bad as Lionel's brother's experience in Winscale, whither he was dispatched in the 1970s to serve as a research radiologist. He had to scrub his children daily when he came home from work and they installed a Geiger counter along with the colour television and fridge-freezer, the latter quite a luxury for Cumbria in 1974.

———

I don't see the point of boxer shorts. No support. And the gap for your sticky wicket, why bother? Too fiddly. You end up groping about for the opening while your fellow man casts suspicious sideways glances. And as my beloved put it, why poke your head out of the window when you can jump over the wall?

———

They didn't like him because he was self-sufficient, which is not to say he was rich because he wasn't. He was just the wrong sort of homosexual. That is to say, close, and mysteriously confident about men and sex, not extrovert, needy, and therefore harmless. I heard the usual stuff, 'it's a selfish life, it's not nice for the children, I have to explain about the strangers going in and out', etc. Did they envy him his solitude and freedom? Do Catholics shit in the woods? He told me a wonderful story once about some man who came round for sex and said, 'Give me a blow job, then.' And Terry said, 'That's not very romantic,' and the man sighed and said, 'All right. Give me a blow job *in the rain.*'

―――

On a less high-minded note, could I put out a call for any unwanted balls of double knitting wool Friends may have? I use them to knit hats for the Sailors' Association which distributes them at Christmas time in their hampers. To all the branches of the Merchant Navy. It doesn't matter if you have odd colours, or not much of one colour and plenty of another: I can do stripes. I used to do jumpers with quite complex patterns but I'm not up to that anymore, so it's hats mostly, because they're really quite simple, and very warm of course. One young man wrote to me to say he'd worn *four* of my hats, one on top of the other, in a storm off Jutland when it was goodness knows how many, some horrific number, of degrees below zero. He'd got some shampoo in the same hamper, which he said was less useful, for reasons the enclosed photograph made clear.

Punks in town could be avoided. They hung around Broadgate and laid siege to the pedestrianised street, especially the Britain in Bloom flower pots outside Littlewoods on which someone had spray-painted the usual slogans. But you couldn't avoid them at school. I like the music now and I'm nostalgic about it because I can afford to be, but it's dishonest of me. Back then it was a different story because I was four foot ten with a bowl cut and a piping voice and I spoke nicely. They were terrifying. The skinheads were the real ones, the real punks, I'm told now, the working-class ones. I couldn't tell them apart from the ones with mohicans. They all scared me. They had streaming colds all the time and they said 'oh, awfully, awfully' and spat at me. There was just one I didn't mind. I'd been cornered on the way home by John Foss and his mates. John Foss's dad was a bus driver and a lunatic. His son's tie was worn fat and short so that it looked like a big cock. I'm not sure if that was the intention. So there I was, shoved up against the wall in the underpass, John saying 'I'm going to pan your head in'. And Chris McAlpine pulls him off me and says, 'He's all right, leave him be. He likes Santana', because I had 'Santana' written in tiny letters on the bottom of my satchel. After that I wasn't quite as scared, and Chris McAlpine even used to nod when I passed him in the corridor, which I found incredibly exciting and moving. It made me feel I'd really arrived, really grown up! Carlos Santana, though. What kind of a punk was he?

I've a choice of two dry cleaners. One is called Fantasy Cleaners, which doesn't inspire confidence. I want to ask: whose fantasy? Mine or yours? The other one is Scorpio – just that, not Scorpio Cleaners or Scorpio Cleaning. The killer in *Dirty Harry* is called Scorpio, isn't he? Row, row, row your boat. Or am I mixing it up with the one with that violent Mafia actor, the one who isn't Clint? He's called Scorpio, I think. *Serpico*. There you go. They're both good films, anyway.

———

Last night I had to sit through an interminable ramble in the Distinguished Lecture series, this one given by a wheezing old Marxist who couldn't read her own gibberish. She had to have seven goes at the word 'deterritorialisation'. At the sixth attempt, she said, 'Oh, please, someone, help me out!' and it was all I could do not to yell 'serves you right'.

———

Success makes you serious – allows other people to take you seriously, I mean. If you try to write a book or paint a picture and you have no luck with it, then the endeavour is always misbegotten, and your work, if that's what it is, becomes an anxious topic of conversation, or is admired with a kind of held breath. No one says, 'Why do you bother?', but that is what they are thinking. Kinder friends, who perhaps turn out to be not so kind in the long run, wish to encourage the attempt, if only to satisfy themselves that they're not uncharitable and that they don't consciously disdain the artistic impulse (although they do, and perfectly consciously, in fact). So they offer congratulations on a great success, when the endeavour is finished, that is nowhere evident. These are the people who appal the artist, who is then obliged to thank them while knowing himself, or herself, pitied. 'I do admire you,' they add, meaning 'I do not admire you. But since you're evidently in the grip of a lifelong delusion, what else can I say?'

———

When you check in, I take a swipe of your card. That's the drill, unless your name is on the prepaid list, which usually means it's a corporate booking. Two gentlemen came in last week. I swiped their cards because they weren't company prepaid and then Mrs Busybody comes over and says, why did you swipe their cards? I'm from the Library and these gentlemen are giving a reading tonight at the Octagon. They're poets. Turns out that it's all been arranged with Angela – she's the hotel manager. I'm just a duty manager. So I ring Angela, get her okay to put these two on the company prepaid list and Mrs Busybody calms down. That night I left instructions for Yuri, he's the night manager, not to take payment from the card in the morning. You can't cancel the record of the card, you see, but you can put a note on the account so that it isn't chargeable. But Yuri forgot and the cards were charged and Mrs Busybody rang to complain and Angela called me in and it got nasty. We're not doing that well. It's always been tradesmen and conferences rather than tourists in Bolton, but with the downturn there haven't been many bookings and we can't afford to make mistakes. No one can. We had to refund each gentleman's card and then it turned out that one of them hadn't been charged after all, so we'd refunded him unnecessarily and Holiday Inn was £109 down on the night as a result. We'd paid him to stay. And guess whose salary was docked? If it was me, I like to think I'd have done the honest thing and put a cheque in the post. I earn £400 a week before tax, working anti-social hours to get a better rate. I have a wife and kids to support. Bolton isn't a bad place. People look out for each other, but there aren't the prospects of Manchester, let alone London. Everyone on my road is struggling now. The high street is all pound shops and currency converters. There's a carpet-tile remnant stockist but that's closing down. And that's the high street.

———

Samuel and I heard this morning that the refugee camp in Tanzania containing our two sons, Amos and Zizwe, is to be closed. The government is closing it and sending everyone in it back to Burundi, where we know that Amos and Zizwe will face great danger. We think of them at this time, and we would ask that you say a silent prayer for them, too.

———

Liz is her name. Ask her about her hip and time her. About thirty minutes, I reckon. The last time I went I could feel her trying to engage me in conversation. 'Is there a problem, or is it a routine check-up, Mr Davies?' 'And how *are* you, Mr Davies?' She wants to be a dentist herself – *your* dentist – and maybe she is, by night, in some dark corner of her mind. She's fairly mad. 'Oh, I laughed when I saw that head rolling across the road inside the crash helmet.' That was Liz, witnessing a serious traffic accident.

––––––

You'll be entering the Olympics, a couple more lengths, won't ya? For the Olympics, I reckon. No? I'm not a swimmer. I'm not much of a swimmer. I've never been out of Australia. So you're from London. Is that where you were born? The West Country. I've been – but not in, not out of here. The Queen lives in a palace, Buckingham Palace, doesn't she? Is that like a castle, where the Queen lives? Is that right? What does she do with all those rooms? Oh. So you can't just walk in and take a look around. I expect it's like the President and the Secret Service. What would you do with so many rooms, anyway? You'd have to have, like, a table in one and a chair in the other. A fork. Or a spoon. But she is rich, isn't she? I bet she is. How do you become a royal person? Could I become, like, a Duke? Duke Michael. Prince Michael. Yeah. You have to be – but then I'd be rich. Except I'm not, that's my problem. I'm extremely poor. Do they still have punk music? Oh, it's over. Are the Sex Pistols still playing? I don't keep up with current affairs. One day I'd like to see London, go there. I've got to get some money together, first. That's what I need. I'm so fuckin' poor.

———

The other side of the street is all families with children and if you don't happen to have children they're just not interested, and I've tried, honestly I have. I've asked questions and shown interest and nothing comes back. As soon as they find out you're childless and single, they glaze over. I did the Street Party for the first three years and that's enough. I made a huge lasagne and offered to help with the barbecue and it was as if I didn't exist. They're all photographers and in marketing at the BBC. I don't think most of them do anything much. It's a mystery. And the *children*. I'm sure they're very nice, but it's the parents who put me off, with their cameras and the endless videos and forced face-painting. 'Look at my children dancing! They're so interesting!' But they're not. And they aren't even dancing, they're just sort of wriggling. You can't escape them in the park, either. They go around in a huge crowd with their kids and colonise the café on Sunday. I can't go there and have a conversation with a friend because it's been taken over by this extended tribe. I'm sure my parents didn't do that. I can't remember having 'playdates', or whatever they're called, and going round with other young families in packs. It's new, and it's outrageous.

———

Wasn't he? He knew all the trains and all the platforms at Flinders Street. Well, I never. Extraordinary confidence. *How* old, did she say? Five? Five. Five *next* September? He's only *four*? That's really . . . quite unusual. His grandparents, they said. Although these days . . . You know, I think I know the man he means at Flinders Street, the one who's nice and helpful, yes. And he's right about the stop, you know, because you *can* walk it from the station. But if I were you, I'd carry on up and then change at Swanston and Collins and get any of the trams going across the city. No, it doesn't matter. They all head in the same direction. It's much quicker that way. Yes. Oh, but *wasn't* he?

———

I went to the Spanking Club once. It was mostly older men in glasses and short-sleeved shirts. A few were wandering around in school uniform, in shorts. The whole place smelt of bleach. On the bar, the organisers, someone, had laid out the implements – gloves, spatulas, ping-pong bats, flails. Knobbly dildos, a few bits and pieces I didn't recognise. People seemed to be enjoying themselves, yes, in a serious-minded sort of way. It was eccentric, I'd say, more than erotic or perverse. Certainly not obscene. After about an hour of leisurely smacking, a skinny little man came in and rang a bell and they served a buffet. The codgers pulled up their trousers, wiped their glasses, and queued for sausages and potato salad, and then disappeared into dark corners with plastic forks and paper plates. No one, not one, washed their hands first. It was revolting.

———

Examples for Quality Aspects of ES2A6. The Lady of Shalott. Normally the bus is full of people chatting, phoning, but in term three there's this transformation and everyone on the upper deck is completely silent and clutching sheets of quotes or formulae in different coloured inks, gently quaking, apart from two spods right at the front talking nineteen to the dozen about Scott Parker and how much they're drinking at the moment. We're all trying to concentrate and all we can hear are these resonant phrases, like 'totally residential area', and I'm still cross because the pony-tailed guy in the queue in front of me landed the driver with a ten-pound note, which held everyone up. And, like, that could have been me, because I only had ten quid, but I bought an apple in Tesco so I'd have the right change, and Hair Despair could've done that, too, only he couldn't be bothered. So. Annoying. That's like a, what d'you call it, the word that means 'perfect example'. Perfect example, yeah. Of how to be totally irresponsible. It's so immature. The spods start talking about some foam party in Leamington, and one of them goes, 'I got Sambuca on someone else and then there's forty minutes before I left I don't remember.' And I think, fuck, can I just walk the rest of the way, please? *The lowest purchase price does not ensure the minimum cost. Nature Poetry.* I seriously need some fresh air.

———

I was prepared to cry over the poor fish and chips. The fish was a square frozen fillet, not fresh, and I kept apologising to David, saying 'I'm sorry. I've made a mistake. We should have gone to the other place.' He didn't seem that bothered, but I know he's got a lot on his mind at the moment and so I tend to inflate the significance of small details, little disappointments. I'm the problem, because I read them all as potential disasters, which I can see isn't very helpful. Anyway, I felt that miserable battered square was a betrayal of what fish and chips ought to be. And when we got down onto the seashore, it was as if the wind had blown away not only my tears but the forty years separating me from my childhood. We walked along the beach to the war fortifications. Mallow grows along the clifftops and blue geraniums. Even from the bottom you can see the bees going wild over them. There's a lover's lane pathway leading up from the rocks to St Peter's Road, and on the steps a peculiar child had written in chalk: 'Mother Mary Is A Spastic. Is Your Mum's Name Mary, or are you just A Moron?' I walked past it as if I hadn't seen it and couldn't stop wondering: who is that child, and what are his parents like? Is he a bully? Mother of Mary, it's a girl, of course! Who is *she* bullying, then? We had time for some tea before the train back and sat at a café table looking down a narrow, half-timbered alley which seemed to end in a wall of choppy green water. I've always liked the sight of the sea between houses. The feeling I have about it is distantly related to the thrill of watching tidal waves swamp city streets in disaster movies. I like the reminder that we're scum on the surface of things, and that out there, not far away, is an irresistible force waiting for us. It should be terrifying, but for some reason I find it very consoling. Some people find the vastness of the sky at night frightening for similar reasons. And I don't. That's what David and I have in common, I think. A tolerance of the big fears. We should have been astronomers.

———

The question of whether or not a machine can write a sonnet or a symphony is not the interesting question. The interesting question is: by whom should such a sonnet or symphony be judged, and how? Turing argued that a machine-made poem might best be appreciated by another machine, and not by a human being. I think what he was getting at is this: AI is bedevilled by anthropomorphism. But it isn't how well machines can do things, from *our* point of view, that ought to concern us. We have to wean ourselves off the idea of estimating machine function as a kind of graded performance, with 'most human-like' as the prize-winning category. Whereas it's the extent to which we are *categorically excluded* from whatever it is machines are doing that matters. When they finally speciate, a fundamental barrier to mutual comprehensibility will exist, in the same way that a species barrier presently exists between dogs and cats or cats and humans. The notion of inter-species inferiority or superiority is ours. It's a category error and has to do with our particular kind of self-consciousness. It may turn out to be lacking in a machine consciousness, which is not bound to carry over into its workings the precisely human operations of the precisely human ego, though that is not to say the machine will be without feelings. It will merely be without *our* feelings. When machines truly start to think, they will be unthinkably different. That is what we have to try, God help us, to grasp.

———

You know you're among the remnants of the aristocracy when you accept an invitation to Sunday lunch in Deal and find yourself talking to a florid character who eats with his mouth open and who, when you turn your ankle on his steps, produces from his 'cold store' a compress made of frozen squirrel.

———

Brenda, at the next desk, is a fairly casual racist. I mean, she's not knowingly a racist, but then that's almost the definition of casual racism, isn't it? She fancies herself as a bit of a singer, too, and I heard her say to Lola, who really is a singer (in a good band, too), 'Don't take this the wrong way, but only black people can sing the blues.' Lola didn't react for a bit. Tap, tap, tap, on she goes. And finally replies, looking down at the keyboard like she's lost something, 'Well, I'm black – and I can't sing the blues.' 'No, love,' Brenda says, patting Lola's arm, 'I'm not saying you *can't* sing the blues – I'm saying you *can*.'

———

No one in the close liked my godfather except the woman he called the coiffed spider, and me. I think she knew he didn't like her. She brought him 'meals on wheels' even though he wasn't an invalid, and when he shouted at her, she just laughed and said, 'I'll come back when you're feeling better.' According to Paul (Paolo Vaissello was his real name, which he changed to Paul Vessell after the war), Mrs Yates did the same for the other elderly residents in Hamer Gardens, looking after them when they hadn't asked to be looked after, probably because she was old herself and this was her way of making it clear that she wasn't *that* old, not like *them*. Or maybe she was genuinely selfless . . . Well, one by one they succumbed to her pot-roasts and creamed spinach, and dropped off the perch. But where they were powerless to resist her, or just too good natured to object, Paul didn't mind telling Margaret exactly what he thought of her. 'You must think I'm rich. I expect you want my money. Well, I *am* rich – but it's all going to my godson, d'you hear? I don't have a family. They're dead, do you understand?' This was in front of me. I was staying for a few days at half-term. And when the spider had gone, he lost his temper. 'Do I have to spell it out, for Christ's sake? Can't she see the statuary? Is she blind?' Paul's garden had male torsos tucked into the borders where one might normally have expected to find gnomes, or indeed borders. I think she was probably a little bit in love with him. He taught music in Bologna after the war. I liked her toffees.

———

We can take that tea-towel back to the city and wash it. I'm particularly fond of it because it belonged to my father and first came to the shack in 1979. What we need, in its place, are some tea-towels to which no one is too attached. I would suggest the little blue and pink jobbies we have at home, but I know for a fact those are Lionel's favourites. And so the search goes on.

———

I saw *ET* again, the other night. Every time I'm in pieces when we get to the last half hour, every time. It's like a religious experience, the confusion in the home, the resurrection, the bikes lifting off and flying across the moon. I can't bear it. And I'm suddenly angry, terribly cross and I go stamping round the room and clapping my hand over my mouth because I realise the neighbours can probably hear. It's because I remember an awful night out with my father, when *ET* came out in the 1980s and I was fourteen. It wasn't cool to like *ET*, really, but everyone did. You had – you *have* – no choice: it's a brilliant attack on adolescent cynicism, apart from anything else, because the elder brother in the film, Elliott's protector, falls in love with ET, too. Brilliant stroke, that. And Dad just dismissed the whole film out of hand, but with this hatred I'd not seen before. He kept saying, 'Some fucking puppet, some rubbery thing', and pointing out how mawkish the whole enterprise was. And I said, 'Well, have you seen it?', and he absolutely went for me. 'No, I fucking haven't,' he said. 'And I don't fucking want to.'

———

I have heard of a being who roams the larger world, listening but not speaking, seeing not being seen. I sometimes think he wants to contact me, us, anyone, to prove he's more than the voice in my head. He's perhaps more like the man in the mirror who goes on watching me when my back's turned. He is one of many, possibly. I feel him searching for a language and a voice behind the surfaces. He does not order me to pay heed or come in dreams, exactly, though to some, afflicted by a different sort of visitor, I dare say the traveller appears that way. Mine asks me. I seem to see his mouth opening, speaking words I can't quite hear, a radio station blurred by static. He asks me to pay him whatever attention I can. He knows it sounds implausible, and that is how I know I am not mad and that he's good. He does not order me to act. He cannot act himself, and yet he's real. He roams the larger world, opening his mouth, listening.

———

We often do video-conferencing with other schools and sometimes the lessons are recorded. They're usually enjoyable. The other day, one of our lot got out of hand. We have several children with attention-deficit problems, you know, and those are often the result of other disorders, so anything in a group is good for them, and rather arduous for the teacher! I played the session back that evening to see how it looked, and I found it quite upsetting. It was the reality of it – the repetition, the hammering away, my voice above everyone's, because there is no other way. This is it. Here we go, this is me speaking:

'We're going to *end* now with Conall. We're going to end – no. That's not what we're going to do, Rahul. We've had a very good debate and you've all raised some interesting points and now we're going to end, we're going to *end*, yes, with Conall.' It's unbearable. I meant it nicely and now I look like I've put him on the spot. 'What did you want to say, Conall? You've been very patient. Now it's your turn. Conall?'

———

Oh, Christ, and the lead is an evangelical Christian, so he treats Trevor and me, and Ray and Maria – I mean, he's really in the right profession, isn't he? – as if we're barely tolerable, tainted. I've got ten weeks of him. The more I think about it, the more it becomes clear to me that evangelicalism is the spiritual equivalent of materialism. It's another kind of complacency – another way in which vain people can enjoy their sense of entitlement without feeling guilty. Stars, eh?

———

Twenty-five years ago, that was my first trip abroad – Sydney to London. I'd bought this lambswool coat which weighed a ton, because everyone said the London winter would be perishing, and I got there and it was relatively mild, and everyone was in jogging bottoms and legwarmers, looking relaxed. And I arrived doubled over with stomach ache because of all the food I'd eaten on the plane. The other thing I had on, under the lambswool coat, was a three-piece suit. I suppose I imagined it was London and everyone – well, I wanted to look my best on the street, didn't I? Lambswool coat, three-piece suit and stomach ache. Oh, and it's so far. At least we've only got to fly to Canberra, which is an hour or so, maybe less. But twenty-six hours, you poor thing. I hope you've had a lovely time. We have, haven't we, Frank? This is our fifth year in Melbourne for the Comedy Festival. And we've seen three comedians, all of whom talked about identity, sex and long-haul travel. It came back to those three things.

———

If the vacuum were not so complete, the sound of every culture speeding by, from bacteria to late macro-sentient galactic entities, would be that of a cistern filling in the ears of the creator, the soft flare of emptiness nixed and life's brief quelling of the silent storm, which rages on and on.

———

The one meeting I had with the studio ended after about thirty seconds. A man whose name I never learnt, because he was a late stand-in for the person we were meant to see, sat down for five seconds, shook my hand, and took a call. 'Got to go,' he said, and pointed at me and at Sarah, who'd set this up. 'I love it. Talk to Linda about everything.' Something in the last word, or about 'Linda' maybe, wasn't right. Maybe the violence happened too soon?

Chronologically it came at the end, but it also opened the film, in the restaurant. Flashbacks, oh dear! Would Linda have an opinion? Who was she? Sarah looked fairly pissed off. How did one find Linda and talk to her? About anything?

———

My brother used to lose his temper and because I admired him in many ways, I grew up thinking this was an admirable, exciting thing to do. What am I angry about? I don't know. It shocks me. It isn't let out of the house much anymore, but occasionally I feel my jaw lock and every muscle in my body stiffen because in my head I'm visiting some awful vengeance on someone. I take a few deep breaths and walk on and maybe catch someone's eye and think: 'They know. They've seen me, but they'll not see me again. I'm okay.' The other day, I'd been angry with my sister, the usual preposterous argument in which I set the world to rights. The flight of fancy crashed when I ran into my next-door neighbour who saw me talking away to myself, and called out 'Having a nice chat, are we?' I texted Teresa in a fit of remorse: *Are you coping?* She looks after patients at home. It's hard work. Unfortunately I was using predictive text. *Are you boring?* was what I actually wrote. She thought it was hilarious.

———

They were a bunch of professionals. Of teachers. There was a geography teacher, a history teacher, and an

English teacher. They were hustlers – that's the point. They'd organised themselves into a group and they went from pub to pub, wiping out. Cleaning up, sorry. They *knew* they were going to win. They'd organised – developed a strategy, so that no one else would have a chance. And they were so smug, that's what got me. You have to understand, it was a calculated play. Nothing innocent about it. It wasn't that they were competitive or that they wanted to win – that wouldn't worry me. It was the fact they were hustlers, and the point about hustlers, the *point* about hustlers you have to get straight is that they *always* win. It's not fair. The locals didn't stand a chance. Those fucking teachers. I could have strangled the lot of them. Don't go thinking there was anything innocent about their plan. A hustler is not what he pretends to be. He starts out being one of you, and then little by little he plays his cards and before you know it you're fucked. They've got dark designs.

———

The poets seem to agree: the great thing in life, that thing that makes us human and therefore moral, is our power of choosing. Deny us that and we become slaves, automata, senile incompetents. The other great thing, they reckon, is being in love. I loved Martin and felt like a revolutionary: it was me against the world! He didn't feel the same way, that was the trouble. I could see that he was continually making the choice to be with me, while I honestly felt I had no choice to make. I'd been lucky enough to come across him and that was that. And when he left people said, 'Remember you've got a choice', but what choice did I have exactly? You could say I chose not to want him to leave me, if you were being heartlessly Californian about it, or you could be honest.

——

Owen stood in the middle of the fuck-joint, almost declaiming. 'It's what people have in their heads, isn't it? They're only doing what they have in their heads. What's the matter with that?' He had that haunted look, I'm afraid, the combined consequence of insomnia and too much weed. I was going to object. I was going to say what you might expect someone to say – 'That's fine, as far as it goes, but what if the fantasies are violent? What if the fantasist has no conception that they're violent?' – and then say, oh, I don't know, that thoughts are neutral and actions moral, thinking while I'm thinking this that Owen is very troubled, when he stared right at me and I realised he didn't have anyone to talk to. And maybe not much sense of what he'd just said. Or: he needed to be contradicted in some way, as if what he was saying was 'Tell me what's wrong with what I've said. Talk to me.' The awful thing was, I couldn't. I thought: he's crazy. This place is crazy. What is that Chinese guy *doing*, crawling around on the floor, getting fucked left, right and centre? If you use a condom and it breaks and you get the post-exposure treatment, the drugs cost £1,000. If you get HIV, the NHS will spend £300,000 on you all told. And if you're already positive and you go around barebacking, that's hundreds of thousands of pounds, millions, you're costing the public service. Hundreds of millions, possibly. I know that's not the whole story. But. So I excused myself and went to the toilet. While I was there, it occurred to me that Owen had been addressing an ideal person, a sort of absent therapist, and I felt sorry for him. Sorry for me, too, later. The toilet was awash. My trainers got soaked and no one would sit next to me on the night bus, which stopped for ages outside the British Interplanetary Association in Vauxhall. Where do they go for their day-trips? That's what I'd like to know.

———

The ferret box had two compartments made from marine plywood and modelled on old pencil cases, the ones with sliding tops. I gave each compartment its own gate at the end. Separate gates are a good idea, because ferrets tend to want to escape as a group. For the shoulder strap I used an old seat belt. When Dad unwrapped it, he said, 'That's handy', and I could see he was pleased.

———

It's as if a skunk went in there, shat itself, died, and the whole lot got turned into a sandwich. And there are queues, that's what I don't understand. Many, many people, at all hours of the day, who want incontinent skunk sandwiches.

———

I still teach at a school for deaf children. I've been all over. I did my training in the Eastern states, in Massachusetts, and then I had the opportunity to come to England. I was looking for somewhere to live and I read an advertisement in *The Times*, put there by Mary Boyd. She said she'd had nineteen replies to that little advertisement but I was the first through the door so she offered the flat to me and I lived with her in Muswell Hill for a while. It was only later, when I was living in Balham, that I thought of ringing her and asking her about coming to Meeting. Westminster Meeting was where I joined. This is a lovely house, here. Toorak is a very peaceful Meeting. The gardens are beautiful, the jacaranda and the Singapore Lady. Tam does the hardy fern display and Betty reads all the way through the Meeting, every week. They're lovely people. I'd come more often but I can't realistically afford the taxi here and back more than twice a month. I get half fares but it's still so expensive. I came back to Australia because my mother had moved into a hostel and she needed my assistance. And I was fortunate to have another eight years with her. I'm in a lovely hostel myself, now.

We didn't talk much, but I did feel close, I suppose. He had a very even temperament, despite the caprice. His actions were prompt, you know, which made them, and him, seem angry, but he wasn't at all. 'That rabbit's getting too fat,' he said one day, pointing to the hutch, and by evening it was in the pot. It happened several times.

'I bought you a rabbit,' he'd say a few weeks later. Or a guinea pig, or a hamster. The guinea pig lived in a Victorian parrot cage, with a door I left open one evening. Well, the ferret got in and I came downstairs to find the guinea pig with its head sort of eaten-out, excavated, like a creme egg. I must have been upset. I don't remember. The thing I couldn't get used to were the sad dogs at Southall Livestock Market. You'd go along and there'd be these whippets and lurchers and collie crosses, dragged around by men in short-sleeved shirts with pierced ears and unblinking eyes. The dogs had 'for sale' signs around their necks. Some of them barked endlessly, at nothing. The others were silent. I hated that almost as much as I hated hurling, and school. I had to go hurling on a Sunday morning, because I was Irish, and Mum asked me if I was enjoying it and I said no, and that was the end of the hurling. I didn't go to school very often, either. The careers adviser asked me what I wanted to do when I left school, and I said I didn't mind. 'Well you must have some idea!' she cried. 'It's important to have aspirations!' 'I didn't say I didn't have aspirations,' I replied. 'I just don't care what job I do.' Bang. Detention. Letter from school. Mum said, 'I don't know what the fuss is about. You answered her questions, didn't you?' Oh, Mum was kind. So was Dad. They were kind underneath, very. Whisper went for my baby rabbits, once. She got through the fence and knocked them about the lawn, and Mum ran out to where there were these pathetic pieces of white scattered over the grass, shouting, 'Don't look, David, don't look!' She picked up the limp bodies and put them in a basket. I think I did cry then. 'Don't look!' But I did, and I pointed, and suddenly there were six little white heads and six pairs of sticking-up ears peeping over the rim of the basket. They'd been knocked out, that's all. She died when she was sixty. She came back from the hospital a few days before the end. They sat on the sofa, holding hands. I took a photo of them and that was one of the photos I thought would be in the safe. Would she have been proud of me? She wouldn't have minded what I did. They didn't need to say the things we say now.

II Where Do You Get Your Tired Ears From?

You can get cut off by a landslide or a fire. A few months ago, a family down at Abbeyard were isolated by a rockfall, but only for a morning. The greater danger, the one big danger, is fire. The fire in 2010 was caused by lightning strikes along the ridge. The fire ignited in three separate locations, united, rolled down the Sugarloaf valley and by the time it got to us it was one giant fireball. It skipped – oil fires crown, which is to say they skip from tree crown to tree crown – and jumped right over the shack. But . . . terrifying, *terrifying*. It's 48 degrees, then 50, then more, and the sky goes black with smoke and you're ringed by fire and the oxygen is being sucked out of your patch by the surrounding blaze and you can't breathe. And the river's no refuge. The water heats up, dries out and the boiling hot sludge coming downstream is full of debris and smoking dead cattle and animals and embers the size of melons and bits of burning tree. You're covered in all the right guards and soaked in flame retardants and you've dug a ditch round the house (if you're lucky with time, and have a digger) and still it's down to pot luck. If you're out of luck, you're out of luck.

———

I'm at this conference listening to a brilliant man talk about Charles Babbage's Difference Engine – the precursor to the computer, loosely speaking. He's describing it as an autonomous construct. I don't know. I thought the rule for something being autonomous, like a kind of life, is precisely that it has to self-start. It has to be original in the sense that it has to be more than the result of an imposed discipline. And by those standards, Babbage's beautiful monster, with all its banks of ante-digital data, is no more a self-starting entity than my laptop. Or my toaster. Byron's daughter called it a 'calculus of the nervous system', which is a great phrase, but . . . you had to pull a lever to get it going. Even now, you have to turn things on, don't you? The cry still goes up: where's the switch? The number of speakers who couldn't work the lights on stage! Or find their way around the desktop. 'Now, I don't quite know what I'm doing here . . . where's the file? I thought I moved it . . .' So, I was feeling stupidly reassured about all this, when I saw my neighbour have one of those old-man coughing fits, you know, with the grisly hiatus between the end-of-the-world expectorations and the gurgled apologies. Professor someone, decorated and retired. I could just see him being wheeled out, packed off in an ambulance. And I could also see some nurse picking up the phone to his wife or one of his kids in the middle of the night, and one of them groping for the light, minutes after having made love, and coming to terms with his death, vaguely aware that everything is held in balance, and all at once I saw that we're not self-starting either, are we? We're not, as individuals, self-organised. Nothing alive is. Something, whether it's sex, or a bolt of lightning, has to get us going. Matter began to twitch billions of years ago, but why did that happen? There's no law of physics saying it has to. Why twitch? Why self-replicate? Why? The leap from the inorganic to the organic – that's the bullet everyone's trying to dodge, isn't it? Where's the switch?

———

When I was a child I didn't have an identity and I didn't want one. I was neither boy nor girl, male nor female. I was just a pair of eyes, a nose, some ears. Receiving the world, the brilliant blue sky, people talking above me.

———

Neal and Ursula are both epidemiologists, which makes it sound like one of them caught it off the other, but they only work three days a week each, and that rather brings them down to earth in my eyes. I suppose you have to hope that the epidemic doesn't strike on the one day they haven't got covered. Anyway, there we were in the shack on a glorious morning, about to have breakfast, and I've put the kettle on and put some tea in the pot, and Neal watches me and calmly picks up the pot and tips the perfectly good dry leaves into the bin because – I imagine, I assume – I haven't warmed the pot first. With less socially awkward companions, and with more of a guiding intuition of their humanity – I'm put off by the little whirrs and clicks coming from their children – I might have pointed out that you warm a ceramic pot, so that it doesn't crack. Whereas aluminium conducts, so you don't have to. 'I'm sorry,' I say. Why do I feel as if I have to apologise? 'I'm sorry – I always use bags at home. I'm lazy, I'm afraid.' And Ursula replies, with a sort of pent-up literal-mindedness: 'Oh no, it isn't laziness. We just prefer loose-leaf tea.' Well, I wasn't saying *they* were lazy, was I? I was saying I'm lazy, although the irony is I'm not.

———

Where do you get your tired ears from?

———

So I go to the conductor, 'Can I smoke on the train?' I'm being polite. Hazel says I'm aggressive but I ain't. Least I'm asking him. Fuck do you want? And he goes, 'Sir. If you smoke you'll be arrested. It's as simple as that. It's as simple as that,' he goes. 'It's been that way for three or four years now. It's a railway by-law.' So I go, 'What if you haven't been in society for three or four years?' and he fucks off down the carriage shaking his head. Nice one. Can't smoke. He'll send me back to prison for smoking. Like to see him try.

———

Here is a famous pub. It's called The Portcullis. Legend has it that one of England's most celebrated poets used to come here and walk around naked. He was well known and liked, though whether or not for his poetry I couldn't say. It also happens to be the former residence of Jacco Maccacco, the Fighting Monkey, who was a draw at fairs across London in the 1790s. Monkeys can be trained to fight, and Jacco was an exceptionally vicious little creature who fought and killed many dogs. Wordsworth mentions him in his correspondence. Well, Jacco was much more famous than Mr Wordsworth. Heaps more. No, I *don't* know who the naked poet was. He came later.

———

Are you still there with me? What I'm going to do is set them on the road to producing some kind of bridge document. They looked at the risk assessment procedure and they were going to refresh all of that. The other interesting thing is asset failure. Transformers that explode or catch fire. And my question to you would be: are there failure frequencies out there for the new gen stuff? What I might do is get tech assurance involved and get yourself and myself, and the tech guys, in a room with Ian Cartwright. Yes. Well, my role is project-based. It started out as process safety but that broadened as soon as the gas component ramped up. It ramps up quite quickly, oh yes. I mean, sure. Ian's got some ideas, but opportunities – opportunities to get involved are legion. Hello?

———

Finally, after months of guilty prevarication, I've read your book of stories. You may remember me congratulating you on it when we met at Dinah's leaving do, but the awful truth is that at that point I hadn't read it at all. I'd bought it – which is something, I suppose. Everything, possibly, to an author (though you must be doing quite well by now? I certainly hope so), but as to actually sitting down and turning the pages – well, *tempus fugit*. They're horribly good, though. Like bronze miniatures: small sketches of domestic living and discontent pressed into some harder surface. Everything is in close-up – the teenagers, the weary mum, the various crises (I loved the hint of rushed cookery) – and then the camera pulls back and we see the characters as they really are, as we are, figurines in a landscape. The effect is disconcerting, quite chilling. I particularly admire the way you achieve all this without resorting to any obvious reversals or twists in the plot. We are not solving equations, as I tell my students. I don't want to see the workings of a story; the trick is to make each logical step in the narrative look and feel like a revelation, consistently and spontaneously true. It's wasted breath, I fear, since like any young mob they are in thrall to the Unexpected. I have tried pointing out that the biggest surprise of all is frequently that things and people really are as they seem. Nobody, in your stories, does anything you would not expect them to. Occasions for learning, self-improvement and moral instruction crop up all the time, but they are resisted. Like Catherine Sloper, your characters can only be who they are. I worried at first that the heroine of 'Split' would feel remorse, or have some inkling that sympathy is an acquired trait and help the screaming child with the raisin up her nose, so it was a relief when she walked away with such joyous unconcern. You touch on a truth that transcends the artistic, of course. The more people know you want something – help, let's say – the less likely they are to want to give it to you. Probably help is only help if it is offered, not sought, though I wouldn't want to press the point.

———

You're a nice, shy person, but you can't be bothered to make an effort on anyone else's behalf. And when someone else does, on yours, you resent it because of the glimpse it affords of a better way of behaving. And, maybe, you see how easy it would be to be a little more considerate, to take the time to phone occasionally, to buy a drink, to come up with a plan for the day or for an evening out, and it amazes even you how much you still can't be arsed. Which means that you know you're also a cunt. Or should I say a troubled but sensitive person – and you rate this self-knowledge. Whereas those who love you, the poor blind, heartbroken, desperate buggers, well, they're not inadequate to begin with, are they? They had the whole world to choose from – and look who they chose!

———

I had an idea you were British. Well, I suppose you could have been North Italian, but no. Actually, I'm here on my own. I was with some friends in Tonbridge – Tonbridge, not Tunbridge Wells, it's seven miles away – and I had to move house and I had two weeks and I thought, where shall I go? I thought, I went to Greece last year and I've

been to Spain and the south of France. I could go to Australia but people go there just to say they've been there,
don't they, so I came here. Fifty pounds return flight to
Alghero. That's not bad, is it? Well, fifty-one with the
visa. I thought about driving down to Cagliari and getting a single flight home but it's expensive. I like Bosa.
Everyone's so friendly. And the palms by the river – it's
tranquil. The cafés. The pink houses. Café culture.

———

To the east, where it's lighter, the edge of the cloud hangs
and drifts in feathery grey clumps. Here at the tea rooms
it's raining as if it has never rained before, as if the past
two months of inundation never happened. How can it
be so new and such a relief? Children defiantly, then elat-
edly, go on playing football in the wild downpour. They
don't think about it. They're ready. They notice, sort of,
that the grown-ups have no control over the weather, and
no control over them because there are babies that need
to be wrapped up, screened off, taken in. Other kids, less
sporting than the drenched semi-pros, but breathless with
the same mad excitement, are practising diving, rolling
around on the grass and flapping their sodden arms. One
wears a plastic cape like a shroud and looks on miser-
ably. He wants and does not want to be wet through, too.
The older mum under the tree struggling with the pop-
pers on her own mac has told him he'll catch his death.
Other children are wet and alive. He turns and walks
very deliberately up the parapet lining the steps. Stops,
looks up. The fatties are clamouring at the cake counter

inside. The thinnies are screaming with delight on the pitch. A little girl in a Fernando Torres T-shirt is laughing toothlessly through rats'-tail hair. Her eyes are wide and bright. Now she is coughing with the effort of laughing, but still jumping backwards and forwards. The boy in the cape joins her. He is much older than her. She is four, maybe less. He is seven. It doesn't matter. They are not related. They do not go to the same school. They won't run into each other until the next time, if there is a next time. Who cares about the future? It's now that counts. It's the most brilliant thing, ever, and it's a puddle.

———

They can't hide who they once were. They can't hide their essential weakness. They want to be other people. I could tell all of that just from the way he said to me, 'Tell us how you did it.' What he wanted to know was: how had I written an exam paper from memory that corresponded exactly to a published essay. I had no smartphone up my sleeve, no access to the web. They weren't interested in the plagiarism per se. They weren't, it amuses me to point out, bright enough to ask themselves any questions about the source I'd supposedly cribbed. It didn't occur to them that the source was me, or that it was part of the set-up. They had no idea. They just wanted to know how I'd remembered such a lot of text and reproduced it exactly. Not nearly. Exactly. 'If you tell us how you did it,' this guy wearing a club tie with a denim shirt said, 'we will pass you.' I shit you not, a tie with a denim shirt. There used to be this kid at my school who made trouble the whole time, but I could throw a cricket ball up in the air with one hand, over my head, and catch it with the other hand without looking up or across, and that used to stop him dead. 'How do you do that?' he'd say. Or even, once, 'It's not fair.' It's not fair! And you know what? It isn't. It is not one little bit fair.

———

Anger and comedy share the same psychology. A comic is funny because there's something in his bearing, his way of thinking and acting, that he can't control. If he learns to control it, he stops being funny. An angry man, in more or less the same way, can't rule his self-disgust. With this further refinement: he lives in perpetual fear of a loss of command that has already happened. Ages ago.

———

I was interested in your remarks on teaching and writing because I was a teacher myself for many years. I was fairly creative before I went into teaching, albeit in the social sciences, and I was very productive – perhaps creative isn't the word (I'm getting on), but certainly *inspired* – again as soon as I finished, and not at all during. What I mean is, I don't think the two ways of being are compatible. And I liked teaching, I did. But nurturing and doing are utterly different. Oh, I know teaching is 'creative'. We're all creative, aren't we? But that's like the sad lady who once said to me 'I'm a nice person, really' after she'd knifed her father. He was a monster and deserved to be knifed, in my opinion, but that's by the by. We're all nice. All creative. I'd get out of it as soon as I can, if I were you.

———

On the second day of the conference, he cornered me and started explaining 'distributed intelligence', which as far as I could see is a dressy term for old-fashioned co-operation – the idea that lots of small computers working away on something are probably going to come up with a solution much faster than one big box of lights. Two hands are better than one, etc. I agreed with what he was saying and he carried on regardless, repeating himself in a slightly peevish way as if I hadn't understood or, more likely, couldn't be expected to understand. 'It's more than that,' he kept saying. 'It's not just that.' 'There's more.' It was peculiar. He seemed to want to hang on to the knowledge – not to distribute it – and then he began coughing again and people started moving away.

———

The man coming through the kissing gate, wearing a fawn polo-shirt with the buttons done up and glasses, carrying a thermos and a knapsack. Shorts and socks. He says 'hello' abruptly, as if embarrassed. Strides off through the corn, head down. When he's pretty sure I'm not behind him, he'll stop at the next stile to take Fitter & Richardson's *Collins Pocket Guide to British Birds* (1966 edition, revised) out of his knapsack and check. That was surely a black redstart he saw back there. Wait a minute. Let's see. The last time he saw one of those was on that walking holiday after A-levels, with Hughie. Must look him up.

———

Carol, who is throwing the memorial party, who is the widow, who is in shock, has been erased from the picture. If you're not a Wilson by birth, forget it. Later, Eric's sister forces everyone to sit through *Reel Guys*, a home-made production about Scott's fishing trips to Canada. Lots of footage of her nephew Scott holding gasping fish by the tail alongside red-faced men in plaid shirts and rubberised clothing. Carol sinks further into the sofa while Mary-Ann Kissane, née Wilson, whom the normally restrained deceased once admitted was 'slow as molasses', sings the praises of the men in her family. Scott loves his Pop, he sure loved his Pop, he knows he had the greatest Pop in the world. In a corner of the darkened room, Ryan, Carol's son by her first marriage to a bisexual composer, talks to Mary-Ann's expressionless husband, who like Ryan works in ER. They discuss scalpels and antimicrobial coatings. 'Y'know, like they use in Guatemala,' says Ryan, and Mary-Ann's husband nods. In five years' time, Carol will admit she hated Eric's dim sister. After many visits to California to see the family who never visited her except that once, in order to treat her like a servant in her own home, she will come, finally, to her senses and call Mary-Ann a piece of work. To her face. But for now she is trapped in front of *Reel Men*, though in some ways glad of the low lighting and terrible film, both of which allow her to cry in peace. And here is Scott now, in person, at the door of his bedroom, which leads off the living room, or one of the many living rooms in this enormous New England house on a hill by a lake – here is the real Scott, a forty-something man in patterned pyjamas, saying goodnight. He is married. His wife, whom he met when she was an air stewardess, wants nothing to do with him anymore. She still flies, still has affairs, and won't hear talk of a divorce. Carol suspects she is one of those liberated open-relationship people who are secretly very afraid of what others think. 'Good night,' Scott says. He is holding an ancient bear.

———

Light noise will rouse me and lull me back to sleep again. When I wake up, the yard outside is wet and the day is bright. I can't put the two together. It feels as if I've forgotten the very thing I swore I would remember. The concrete is greening where moss is creeping back around the drain, under cover of ferns. The back of the house creates shade. The front blinks. I have been on my own for days now, looking out of these windows, rubbing my eyes, wondering if I ever had plans for a life like this. I notice drops of water hanging off the washing line. It comes to me like a secret affirmation, whatever it was, and I'm relieved.

———

In the entrance hall of the botanical gardens in Berlin stands a cross-section of *Sequoiadendron giganteum*, that long-lived and quintessentially 1970s tree. They had one in the park back home. When it died, the council decided that it should be left standing and turned it into a truly hideous totem pole, as a memorial. (To what? No one knows. The 70s were like that: garish and vague.) Looking at the growth rings of the Berlin slice, I realised that this specimen put on its greatest mass, grew most vigorously, between the ages of 200 and 400. It took two hundred years to get going. Or, for those two centuries, in the plant's ripe and hale middle age, the conditions were optimally good. How I wish the same were true for me.

———

Time kills everyone, of course, though none so literally as my ancestors, the Gais of Bristol, who died of mercury poisoning. John Gai licked into a point the little brushes with which he used to paint mercury onto his watch faces. He would have kissed Sophia, his wife, many times. They had five children.

———

The doorstepping when someone's been killed and you have to let the parents know is one thing. I've learnt to, well, not get used to it – I expect it to be hard, I suppose. You go off from one of those and you're like this, 'now breathe out'. I can feel my chest aching from holding my breath, taking short breaths to get the words out. Then there's the lighter side of life, isn't there? Like, I had to knock on this lady's door last week, because both her neighbours were complaining about the racket she made during sex. The insulation in the Dene isn't – well, there isn't any. She was a nice lady, listened politely and all that. I said how we were sorry to be bringing it up, and she said, 'It's quite all right officer, I understand.' So if you and your boyfriend could maybe keep it down a little . . . She said, 'I don't have a boyfriend.' Girlfriend, then, beg pardon. And she shook her head, and smiled. Very civilised. 'Just me, officer.'

———

The two kids, on the other hand, have inquiring minds. We were playing a game of Either/Or. You have to express a preference, no matter how ridiculous the two things are. That's the only rule. It started sensibly and boringly, knife or fork, hats or scarves, and so on. Neal after a glass of wine said 'RNA or DNA?', which I could see he was very pleased with, and I tried not to sigh. He'd turned the choice into a test, as usual. Which isn't what the game is about. It's a game, Neal, you know? But I was the stranger, the interloper. I couldn't say anything directly, could I? Ursula sat there, drinking a foul-smelling tisane, and after a while said, 'DNA. Of course.' Meanwhile the wind and the rain (wind or rain?) were getting up. There was thunder or lightning and Bethany, who's quiet as a mouse, started giving free rein to her vivid imagination. 'Would you rather be attacked by a duck the size of a horse,' she said, 'or attacked by fifty duck-sized horses?', and I chose the fifty duck-sized horses, because you could always beat the critters off with a big stick whereas a duck the size of a horse would have a hell of a beak. Ursula told Bethany not to be stupid, and Karen, siding with her mother, came up with 'Stars or planets?' The game petered out after that and Neal and Ursula began discussing what Karen would do with the shack when the responsibility for it was hers. In the future. Karen's fourteen and very self-assured, tall, curvy, with straight black hair and large eyes a little puffy from study and reading. She tends to boss her younger sister about and calls her 'my second in command'. She was going on about renovations and fishing and in a lull I said to Bethany, as an aside, 'I expect you have your own plans', to make her feel included. Bethany confirmed that she did and Karen asked what they might be. 'They wouldn't be plans if I told you about them in advance,' Bethany replied, witheringly. Ursula thought that sounded like a threat and Karen said lightly, 'Then in that case I'll have to kill you.' Bethany never took her eyes off me. 'Plan or kill?' she said. Always plan, I said, and she nodded.

III   We Are Prey

I wouldn't be without him, of course. Today we drove out across the Pontchartrain Bridge to the north shore. Vera's, it's a wonderful seafood restaurant. I had the gumbo and Curtis had the blackened catfish. He said I should 'get wild' and go to Bourbon Point. Well, be that as it may, on the way back we took a detour to the NASA facility, where they have the *Saturn 5* first-stage rocket on its side, like something from a giant forest? A petrified forest. They never used it, or we wouldn't be able to see it. Five massive burners out at the back and all that rigging, all the pipes and bolts snaking around the base of the rocket. I started to wonder what the moonshots had been for – and then I chanced to look up, and there he was, the man in the moon, staring down at me between two of the burners. I'm not saying he hasn't many, many faults, but he's happy and that's all that – and he's reliable, except – *here* he comes! Moose! Moose! C'm here! Moose isn't my dog, you understand. I'm *his* owner.

———

I've been involved with clinic defence for years now. Agitation is flaring up because two fundamentalist activists have just been released from jail. One guy was locked up for non-payment of child support. He doesn't believe in birth control or after-care, apparently. The other is Randall Terry, the diehard who sent the President an aborted foetus in a pickling jar. Right. And they want the clinics closed down, that's what Operation Rescue is aiming for. Actually I think they want us all dead, but you know, start small and work your way up. I have some OR next door, which is okay. I haven't spoken to most of my shitface neighbours in years. Why? Because they're all white supremacist bigots! Lady called out to me this morning, after I was on the news. She leant over the fence. 'Pleee-ase, Marmeeee! Don't murder meee!' But my daughter was killed by a drunk and my son raped on a St Louis wharf, so I don't care.

———

The road to Emmaus, ladies and gentlemen, is a very boring walk. Luke said it was seven miles from Jerusalem, about which there is some scholarly dispute. What he didn't say is how boring those seven miles are. A stranger comes along and alleviates the boredom by engaging Cleopas and friend in conversation. Nobody would think there's anything very unusual in that. They get to talking about the death of the Galilean preacher and the stranger asks them who this preacher was. Well, Cleopas must have thought his new friend had crawled out from under a stone. Jesus was the *talk of the town*: everybody knew about this man and how his death had been signalled with strange meteorological events. But did Jesus reveal himself to them? No. I guess he used what we could call the

Socratic method: he asked a question, ladies and gentlemen, because sometimes the lord Jesus, the risen lord, has to probe. No lights out of a sky. And the two travellers were downcast. They stopped in the middle of the road and looked very sad. Like they'd lost their one hope.

———

I'm a Leo. So you're skinny now and you walk and bike, but it's a losing battle, man, and come forty you're gonna be an old man. Like I'm saying, all you need is four hours a week. You can carve four hours a week out of your schedule, and when you're seventy you could be like you're forty and people will go: wow, *I* wanna chest and abs like that guy. And you're desirable, man, cause bottom line is – you're fat and 250lbs and who wants you? It's miserable. Twenty years' time, everyone's gonna be doing weights. We haven't begun to see the tip of the – and y'know, it isn't just a physical thing, it's mental. You work out, you release all those endomorphins, you're fired up and your mental capacity is greatly enhanced. You sleep better, I'm a light sleeper, but you dream better and you wake up feeling great, like let's *go*, instead of opening your eyes and thinking, uh-oh, gravity. You may think you're alert now, but just start doing weights and watch your horizons expand. I haven't done weights for four months but I've still got a great body, see? All you need is some pumpin' and musculature and people will be all over you, man. You stand up like this, instead of all hunched over, like this. That's what I tell Darryl but he doesn't listen.

I've been a member of the League of Women Voters, who were, well, mostly suffragettes and educationalists, for many, many years. Since I was in college in the 1940s. And I belong to the Unitarian Church. I remember the race riots and segregation very well. We fought to keep a school open that white parents had boycotted because of colored admissions. And in '62, our church was bombed for supporting educational integration and the ministers threatened. My husband was set up by a local racist who rang pretending to be the husband of one of my teaching colleagues, and he expressed concern about me. Which was a threat. I got a note through the door late one night that said, 'What would you do if you had five minutes left to live?' Mike and I used to drive the kids to school who couldn't get here on segregated buses. Y'know, and people were murdered for less. That was what it was like, and everything continues. These streetcars were the same then as they are now. They still use sand to brake the cars and the St Charles depot has to cannibalise other vehicles across the country for the right parts. There's a city preservation order on them. Mike used to read aloud 'The Adventures of Isobel', do you know that poem? 'Isobel, Isobel, didn't worry, / Isobel didn't scream or scurry. / She washed her hands and she straightened her hair up. / Then Isobel quietly ate the bear up.' I love that poem.

I had an experience when I was I guess seven – eight? – that I've never forgotten. I heard Psalm 23 for the first time and I could not get the last line out of my head, 'And I will dwell in the House of the Lord for ever'. Not for forty days or forty nights, not for a thousand years, but for *ever*. That was it. It did something to me. I went to bed terrified: it was like I'd been injected. I was going to be imprisoned, and this was a good thing? It was the idea of being inside a house for ever. First dream, I saw my sister at the end of my bed with a big net on the end of a pole. I said, 'Linda.' She smiled back at me and that was the end of that. Then, second time, I heard this man's voice saying 'In a moment you will be introduced to someone', and I held my breath. Same voice said, 'You know who he is, don't you? I'm going to introduce you to the Devil. He's just coming', and I waited some more. Then right inside my head, closer than ever, the deepest, realest voice said 'Hello Darryl', and he knew my name and I woke up.

———

We took some stuffed-shrimp po-boys and went out to La Branche and paddled deep into the reserve. The fireflies were on and off like landing lights and tracer fire and I love it there but I was still on the look-out for two pink eyes, close-set. They're hard to come by, but if you do, the best thing is to paddle past as swiftly and as silently as possible. I was doused in insect repellent because I react badly. Allergies build up. You have like a tank of resistance and when it gets full, you start to react. Anyway,

I'm covered and Mike isn't because the bugs haven't begun to breed in earnest yet. It's only March. We take a
turning into a deep swamp, out of an ox-bow lake, and
eat one of the po-boys by one of Mike's landmark trees.
Bullfrogs, crickets and toads. And then a marsh-frog puff-
ing out its throat in the middle of a cypress shoot. Mike
takes us further into a low thicket overhung with creeper
and Spanish moss. I was quiet as could be but Mike was
quieter, his paddle slipping in and out of the water without making a sound. I was holding the bicycle searchlight
but the marsh-gas has its own luminosity. Then Mike
slaps himself, some giant bug, and I reach forward and he
tips the canoe right over and all of a sudden we're in the
water and *we are prey*.

What did I want in New York? I got tired of being able
to touch everything everywhere I went, like *this*. What I
paid for a one-bedroom apartment I pay here for a three-
bedroom house with a two-car garage and a big garden.
But that took time. When I first got here, man, I could
only get arrested, you understand me? I came to Tulsa,
why. Well, I had a girlfriend who moved back here and
when I showed up and rang her from the station she almost fainted on the line, so that was a big mistake on
my part right there. I was here and I was lost, no money, tired. I remember I caught a bus out to South Lewis
51st. On the map there was a Comfort Inn on 47th and
Yale, except there was no through route to Yale and I
had to trudge along the 51st Interstate. And it was much

further than I'd anticipated. Mistake No. 2: I approached a woman for directions and she ran for her car, got inside, secured the windows and waved me away. Like this, go away, go away, go away big black man. I was mouthing, 'All I want to do is ask you a question.' And she was, 'Go away, I don't want to know.' But that's the thing, there. You have a house, you have direction. You have a place to go. Motion towards. You have nowhere to go, conversation is aimless.

———

Now is really not a great time to visit Oklahoma City. Everyone's kinda moving about in a daze and we're all so distraught. I'm sorry. I know where the NW39th Expressway is, at least I've driven on it. Somewhere nearby? No, I don't have that information . . . oh, a hotel. Now wait a minute. This is so dumb, I can't seem to find . . . The Westside Y. Well, I know that's over on Martin Luther King. You can try them, sure, but it's in a black part of town. I don't know if that matters to you. You – you don't have a car? You're on foot? Without a car?

———

The last time I took the bus I was sat next to this Mexican guy down from Missouri, with a home-cured pheasant. And he was waving this bird around, saying 'See! See! It's not alive!' Right about after that I stopped my wandering. I'm not saying it was, you know, related. I'm not a racialist. This is a freedom we got here, supposedly.

Even with all that you read and see and hear. But I got this sore chest. I got swollen glands and a bad head, and I'm not going to a doctor. I don't believe in them. There's only one doctor I believe in and if he's not gonna cure me, nothing will. He stopped my drinking, helped me quit cussing and beating up on my wife. I expect a miracle. Absolutely. Yes I do.

———

Josephus speaks of an Emmaus about four miles from Jerusalem. It was chosen by the Roman Emperor Vespasian as the site for a colony of soldiers in AD 70. But it's also identified with the modern Qaloniyeh because that name seems to be a corruption of the latin *colonia*. And in Maccabean times, Amwas, which is fifteen miles from Jerusalem on the Jaffa Road, was known as Emmaus. Before it became Nicopolis. That's chapter and verse on Emmaus. You're welcome. Well, I had a good education. Oral Roberts University was very rigorous and well equipped. In 1977, it had an online database from which students could access any class. How many other institutions had that kind of facility?

———

I don't think it's funny, no. And I don't think it's polite to invite someone into your house so that you can ridicule their beliefs. Cheap shots don't make your opponents cheap, you know. The Church of the, what, Revolving Door? But it doesn't even make sense. Oh, I get it. Okay.

Open. Very clever. Look, I'm not here to deny the challenges, okay. I readily concede – I – yes, for those of us who grew up in conservative homes, it's difficult at best. I have to be a good Catholic to someone who's Hispanic and dying from AIDS, I have to able to minister to his family, if they're around. Or they may be Pentecostal, whatever. We are struggling against doctrine in so many ways. But against the far Right the unspoken truth is that we are winning. They want to attack us for our lifestyles but it's a difficult stance to maintain. And they can't dismiss us as an irrelevant cult or anomaly because we're bigger than 99 per cent of all churches in America. And do they *not* want lesbians and gay men to go to church?

———

'A very gracious Texan woman, a prominent club member' – they don't say what club, I notice – 'stopped in for a drink at a soda fountain accompanied by her small daughter. She ordered Dr Pepper for both. "Because," she said to a friend at the same table, "I have seen the factory, the water, the fruit juices and the same kind of sugar I have on my table and I know it is healthful for my child."' I think it's kind of a shame that all the ads mention fruit juices but Dr Pepper doesn't actually have any. Maybe it did back then, I don't know. The water part is quite true, though. Waco has a number of artesian wells. And one 'crazy' well, so called because it is supposed to have cured a woman of her insanity. But the story I like best is the one about Lyndon B. Johnson, who had a vice-presidential edition of a hundred bottles specially made, and they were supposed to be used for the first time during a visit by President and Mrs John F. Kennedy, scheduled for the evening of November 22, 1963. Oh, look. 'If Atlas were on earth, he would recommend Dr Pepper. It is liquid sunshine.'

———

Do you know where I can get a steak and some eggs? Where there's a grill? Are you not from around here? I'm hungry. Yes sir. That would be appreciated. You not from around here? I just got discharged from the Fort Sam Medical Center. I have had various bits of me taken out over the past five years. To stop the cancer. To arrest the spread of it, and now I'm hungry, spite of the fact I have only half a stomach. And one lung. I have one lung. 165 stitches right across my abdomen. The cancer took a hold during my poker-playing years. I was on four packets a day and two quarts of whisky. That's enough to embalm you.

———

This was our schoolroom from first to sixth grade. As you can see it's half-demolished, those window frames had pretty paper blinds to keep the sun out. Look at it all! All crumbling and those foundations. Like bad teeth. I can't hardly bear to look at it myself, but I'm drawn. Every time I come back. My cousin took me in when my Ma died. Pa died before I knew who he was, when I was a baby. I come back to see proud Lillie. She says there's some graffiti somewhere about with her name on it but I've never seen it. The descendants of the Indians still live nearby in conditions of direst poverty. Other of the missions you got wrecks of cars, here you're lucky if you find a tire and a plate. Find all kinds of things, lumps of fur look like roadkill that get up and walk! Either that or there's a mean dog waiting for you behind a fence it can jump. I was lucky. My cousins loved me. I know that for a fact, and that's not always true if you're mestizo in a Hispanic-white family, and you're brought up the only one who is because of some unspecified encounter no one really wants to go into anymore. You're either above or below the rest of the family always. It happens though and I'm the proof of that. I got a good education and I went to law school and I live well.

———

I'm an ex-Jew Catholic convert and my wife Kris is from Uruguay. She's not too happy about my shift in orthodoxies and I'm none too clear about it myself. I can see some kind of logical fallacy, certainly. If the commandment says 'Honour thy father and thy mother', then I guess that means I should have stayed Jewish. At least I waited until my father was dead before converting. I'm a geologist for the government and I'm researching a nuclear facility near Los Alamos. It's amazing how you can do this technical thing and still have these ideological disputes with colleagues who are highly respected geologists in their own right but creationists at the same time. I am in an awful way with one guy, whom I like very much as a person. But he is obsessed with explaining away everything as a Biblical relic. So, all the limestones from here to the canyon are carbonates that were reworked by the Flood, okay. He has nothing to say about the classic reefs that show up here. He is in total denial that New Mexico had any kind of coastal environment. It's crazy. And the dinosaur tracks in the Mesozoic rocks? How can they be late in the Flood like he says? I thought everything outside the Ark was supposed to be dead. Being a Jew Catholic sometimes feels like the least of my problems.

———

The Cross of the Martyrs is a peculiar memorial. It's supposed to commemorate the Franciscans who were killed in the pueblo revolt of 1682, though no one feels that sorry about them now. I mean, it doesn't – well yes, it's awful, but is it really that unreasonable to suggest the Church had it coming? And the plaques on the way up. One is for a pastor who was kidnapped and killed in 1892, and another celebrates New Mexico's native heritage. I don't know. I think I like the graffiti on the picnic tables better. 'Amerikka – Land of the Nobody'. 'Take A Stand – Rich People Are Running Our State'. And how about this one, I like this: 'D.A.R.E – Drugs Are Really Excellent'. Someone's added, 'I know'.

———

Body Electronics is a holistic protocol with meditative technologies and nutritional programs. There's a seminar

I attend every Thursday evening. Geoff's an inspirational teacher. Everyone loves Geoff. He's one of only two BE teachers in the States. We start with the anointment, which is where you rub non-alcohol-based peppermint extract on your temples to facilitate concentration and ward off negative thought patterns. Then we get into the discussion, which is another means of transcendence. So the great thing about BE is that you don't just realise the beauty of each instant, you actually get to live for ever. We have four bodies: physical, mental, emotional and spiritual. And death is a state of mind that the rejuvenative mental body can overcome. Here's hoping! I – I do think I have a different perspective to the other members of the group, yes. Well, I have a different set of expectations you might say. It's just the niceness and the calm I value. I mean, I have objections to the immortal part of it because I don't see what it can do about sudden death – plane crashes and earthquakes and wars. I don't see how I can rejuvenate if I'm in a hundred bits and pieces. And if we're immortal why are we all different ages? But I don't want to pick holes. It's the feeling of being in a group of nice people. I feel safe. And feeling safe and calm is a great analgesic by the way. My parents are on the East Coast, Westchester. It's hard for them. And I get everywhere on my own and for as long as I have left I choose this. This is my car. It was nice meeting you.

———

We're 7,500 feet above sea level and I call this the land of Plenty. Valley is really the wrong word as you can see.

What we're looking at is a pastoral plain torn in two by the Rio Grande gorge. We're over on Ranchitos Lane. I'm native and I've known my neighbours all my life. I went to college in California, came back and met Blake in the Peace Corps. Now we're part-time school-workers. I'm a careers counsellor for teenagers in remote rural communities and Blake works with the educationally disadvantaged and emotionally, uh, distorted on outward-bound projects. We have our own wood-burning stove. And lots and lots of axes.

———

I punish the saint. It is like a punishment until the thing happens. You can pray to the idol for health, harvests, prosperity in the normal way, but if misfortune occurs we go like this, and this, and *this*. The saints are walled up by mothers if their sons are missing or get kidnapped by Indians. When I was little I knew a shepherd boy who disappeared for nearly a year and his mother had a wooden saint for the safety of her son. She buries the effigy. One day she hears knocking behind the plaster and her saint falls out of his place in the wall. The next day her son returns home. I like this punishing. It goes back a long, long way. I descend from the Penitentes, originally. We no longer beat ourselves with sticks – but still we have visions. God is everywhere. Our Lady of Guadalupe, the local shrine, remembers the woman who saw Christ in a tortilla. And the church was moved. A farmer found a saint in his backyard. He took it to his church and gave it to the priest. In his field the next day he sees the same image staring up at him from the dirt. Eventually – this goes on for many weeks – they move the church to his fields because it is a sign the building belongs there instead.

———

I do miss home terribly, particularly Margaret. We were very close. But on the other hand I'm still vastly enthusiastic about everything I love here, particularly my work – experimental psychology, they may call it something else now, I don't know – and the value of the *culture* and the land itself, of course. That enormous long strip of water boiling away at the bottom. Isn't it extraordinary? It never ceases to amaze me. But out here is what we call the valley proper, you see. Yes! We did it all ourselves. And look at the ceiling, and the walls. Genuine adobe. Feet thick. Well, the Spanish are pretty useless at everything, really, but they have managed to keep their religion pure, and that's what I like.

———

My ex-husband lived on floor eleven when we met. I was on floor twelve, but there was a public phone on the floor below. In fact it was in the elevator that I met Mike. I'm sure it was an elevator because when I got in I was on floor eleven and when we got out we were in the car lot. There seems no other reasonable explanation. And we were married and had sweet Jessie a year later.

———

Or what? Revolutionary mystics in the Middle Ages thought all Jews were child-killers. Demons, Herodian Demons. If you're really surprised when I say to you the abortion issue and anti-Semitism are inextricably linked, if you're convinced it's a slander, then read some fucking history. But you've taken a leap of faith, I can see that. That's the trouble. 'I'm not the one who needs to feel shame.' Yes, you are. We do, everyone. You're so confident that all that can be said about God has been said already that you don't open a book apart from the one you're least equipped to read. Look, really look, at the people doing the accusing. Look at where they come from, who they admire. You've made a choice. You're so sure. So unnaturally sure. You know they've done tests on depressed people, people like me who are depressed by people like you, and you know what they found? People who are depressed are the realists. We give a speech, write an article, we know we're fucking losers and half the audience is bored and the other half are pissed off in some private, resentful way, think they can do better. You get up, full of fucking can-do and clap your hands while your pastor fucks little black boys and you say fuck Islam, fuck everyone, fuck the gays, fuck the free press, fuck it all just give me my fucking donuts and insurance. And I'm the baby-betraying coward. Because I don't shoot doctors. You're fucking *insane*.

———

Some people overstate everything, but you can get a long way by sounding as if you know what you're talking about.

Me, I just think life is precious and that we shouldn't seek to curtail it, and that art and shared interests and laughter and the imagination can sustain it. And the truth, certainly. But not held on to, not kinda grabbed, do you know what I mean? I think the balance of probability is – if the deer on the plain hears a rustle, it knows. The instinct is trained. Of course the rustle may be a rabbit not a lion, but the deer has no pride. It can take being wrong, and so can I. I'm wrong about just about everything.

IV Radio Traffic

Everything's still. From the ground floor I can see rabbits, nibbling at the grass growing between the cobbles, and bats. A big silver birch stands in the middle of the court-yard, with a left-leaning branch that threatens to over-balance the whole tree. To keep its balance, the tree will have spread roots in the opposite direction, which is bad news for the flats on that side. There are mosquitoes (the bats' food) and sparrows in abundance; a woodpecker in a garden nearby; housemartins in Treptower Park, darting and swerving over the unvisited memorial. The leaves on the birch are motionless as a photograph. The lights are on in the flats. A lady sits out on her balcony four floors up, talking to a man in the apartment. Voices carry and fade, carry and fade. He agrees with her, I think. I can't see him, but I can see the smoke coming from her mouth, the fruit bowl on her sideboard. It doesn't last long, this part of the evening. Two cigarettes at most.

———

Welcome to the new Greyhound. You may not take hot drinks on the bus. Sushi Zone. I need to pee. Like, it's a special zone. For sushi. *Sorry, we're closed! Only ticketed passengers beyond this point.* Two hours to Chilliwack?

What is this, the All-Hillbilly Tour? *9.30 a.m. departure SOLD OUT. Coffee so fresh you'll want to slap it!* And the hotel stung us for Parking Tax. We don't have a car. I said that. I told them, we don't have a car. How can you, when the car doesn't exist?

———

I wrote about the reproductive system of the stoat for my Biology GCSE. The male grabs the back of the female's neck during sex and this assists ovulation. My answer was illustrated. I got a C. I think it's fair to say that my school wasn't geared towards the sciences. Besides, we had a miserable-looking biology teacher who was having some sort of an affair with the geography mistress. He used to slope into lessons, holding a mug that had a cartoon of a grinning horse on it. The horse was captioned: 'Smile if you've had a bit lately'.

———

A lion on the loose in Clacton, I know. I nearly wrote a letter: 'What, again?' Who comes up with these hoaxes? Why do people believe them? Don't they know what a lion looks like? Can't they tell the difference between a creature that's two feet long, like a cat, and one the size of a car? I'm baffled. It's about as convincing as putting a couple of pyjama cases in the enclosure at Regent's Park. But that's the allure of the Great British Predator for you. Every county has one. And it's always feline. Whereas not five minutes down the road, in a bungalow in Frinton, at least you may be sure to find a *real* Burmese python called Sukie, who is often in the garden at weekends. Escape? Why would she? Rats on tap, someone who loves her *and* a moat. Luxury!

———

Plato says, 'A thing is not seen because it is visible, but conversely, visible because it is seen.' We might also say that a thing is not unseen because it is invisible but rather invisible only because it hasn't (yet) been seen. And merely because a thing is unseen doesn't mean it isn't there. In order to see it properly, you may find that you have to look away. Some things do not like to be observed too directly. Staring fixes them and creates a blind spot. At night, if you want to know whether or not a dark shape is an animal, you must seek out its movement in the periphery of your vision. The same principle applies in relationships. If you want to know what someone's like, don't, do *not* ask. Leave them be.

———

The rocks are bearded with dead moss. They're black – they look blackened, but it is drought that has darkened them, not fire. Snowberries, bright huckleberries and Michaelmas daisy cling to the fine sand above the gravel bars, and from the banks of Dogwood Road you can watch the Fraser river sweep past, the hospital green water clayey and vaguely opalescent, its circular eddies rising, spreading, quietly lethal. The river is still deep, for all the dry weather, and fast. A lone gull beats its way upstream. The poplars on the far shore are losing their leaves, trying to conserve water. Rain should fall throughout the year, but this July and August the clouds haven't come together. Shadows pause in the firred valley and no big storms come. Mornings see the largest avian predators, vultures and bald eagles, circling the Canadian National Railway, and the smallest migrant pollinator – a Rufous hummingbird – suspended in a blur of wings at the window. The small bird will soon be heading back to the Sierra Madre in western Mexico. Folklore has it that these inch-long visitors hitch rides on the backs of geese flying in the same direction, but in this case folklore is wrong. Said to be wrong. They breed in British Columbia and winter in the south. Maybe they follow the gold.

———

I love to travel. I've been all over Europe. Greece, Italy, Spain. Spain I wouldn't bother with again. It's dirty and no one speaks English. England, too dreary. I lived in Switzerland for a year. I like to be spontaneous. Like, three weeks with my mother is enough. So I say to her, 'Mum, I'm going to Banff.' Just like that. That's what I'm like. I get up and go. Like I always say, you gotta *get* to get to where you're going. Banff is full of Filipinos now. (Where do *they* come from?) Oh. No. I've been married for years. He's in Australia. That's where we live, normally. He's there and I'm here. Yeah. What can I tell you? You, though. You got no wife, no ties, you got no mortgage. You're Mr Lucky ain't you? Mr Lucky Lucky. I can't travel as much. I used to travel a whole lot more than I do, but I'm getting old. I visit my mother once a year. It's plenty. It's fine. Man, I have *heard* her Princess Di conspiracy theories so many times. And you know what? I think she's dead. I think she got drunk, got in the car, had a wild old time, and plain screwed up. She's dead. What about you? You lost your driver's license? How long? Eight months. Huh. So you're done. Almost. Shit, it happens. You don't need to tell me. The things I did when I was young, it's a wonder I wasn't put behind bars. That was a long – shoot, now you're just being kind.

———

'Depression, anxiety, bereavement, obsessive compulsive disorder, anger management, low self esteem, irrational fears, *addition* problems, attention deficits, couple counselling, gender etc.' Etc.

———

Cara used to work for me. She had a fairly low-level investigative role in immigration – she was a case-worker for TEFL fraud, which means she got sent out to those fly-by-night international schools of English to see which were even attempting to teach something in return for their hugely expensive student visas. I got suspicious when she didn't turn up a single instance of sharp practice in a year and I called her in. I said, Cara, I can't believe that the 'Wardour and Soho Academy of English', as it calls itself, in the middle of Chinatown, is a legitimate educational institution, and she said, it depends on what you call an education, doesn't it? So I let her go, I'm afraid, but went along to the premises myself, my curiosity a little piqued. And of course the 'Wardour and Soho Academy', which enrolled five hundred students a year, was an un-furnished room full of boxes of paper towels and prawn crackers above a restaurant. Its only occupant was an old man with long white-blond hair seated in one corner at a tiny desk turning the pages of a Boden catalogue. I in-troduced myself and said, where are all the students? He said they'd gone to the library. What about the desks, blackboards – the classroom? 'They've taken everything with them!' he replied, waving his arms. When do they get taught English? 'They learn on the job,' he shouted. 'It's the best way!' And funnily enough, once I'd thought about that, I had to agree. I rang Cara to apologise and offered to reinstate her. But she wasn't at home and a few days later, while I was walking back to work from lunch in Marylebone, I saw her in a suit coming out of the Chinese Embassy.

———

If people like something or think it's good, then they'll tell you. If people think it's patchy but promising or would be okay with changes, then they'll tell you. If the patient is dead, no one says anything. Sometimes the people are themselves dead and you are discouraged for no reason. No one will tell you they are dead. No one knows you're a master of your art, especially not you. You burn all your stuff, thinking 'I'm no good. They hated me', not realising that the silence, in this case, wasn't a verdict. When your stuff arrived in the post, they were already incapacitated at the bottom of the stairs and in no position to judge. They said nothing because they could not speak. The silence was – is – long. You are the more deceived. Possibly they thought 'Now this one, there's something about the sound of *this* one, the noise it makes' as it dropped onto the mat, as they fell in a heap, spines corkscrewed, necks awry. It is an injustice you cannot conceive. The people are dead and undiscovered in a shocking flat. With a bitter hindsight of which you are not logically capable, you might think 'serve them right'. Even this much is denied you. The silence is total.

———

Is it in the nature of small-world bohemians, with a private income they keep very quiet about, to be clumsy in their search for the authentic? I mean, if I were an 'artisan sake maker', would I want to set up shop right next to a cement works? Come to that, what do the cement workers feel about it?

———

It's a lovely new concourse, considering the IQ of some of the people who built it. One of our cleaners, Nagib, worked on site throughout the rebuild and he says a mate of his fell into the foundations when they started on the high-speed link and the constructors paid the police not to investigate. Just remember that next time you're complaining about the price of a teabag at Delice de France. It's all much lighter and you can even understand what's being said because there are hundreds of angled speakers to reduce reverb, and the sentences are broken up with pauses after the consonants. The departures are done by the lady reading the timetable with a gun to her head. She's real, I've met her. I know she sounds synthesised, but she's not. Her name's Lorene. Very nice, tiny person. It's related to Laura, Lauren. She did *The Bill*, though there's no way she'd be an officer in real life. My cousin's in the Met and he's 5 foot 8, and that's on the short side.

———

The director is beginning to lose control, I fear. Last week in the pub she told me that she wasn't so keen on Shakespeare's verse. This week we have a movement workshop and a voice workshop but no actual rehearsals for the third act of the play. We open at the end of next week. And today, while I was preparing to tell my brother – lovely Simon Ridgley – that he was born in the gutter and that that was where he'd end up, in the gutter, Yolande stopped me and said, 'Lennie, I need you to *screw your physical resources up to such a pitch* . . . you can just . . . *dissolve.*' I'm working on that. Meanwhile I have East London to perfect. 'You must be taking Thespis, my son.' Oh, and the dangerous lady novelist whose work we are adapting – she came in yesterday. Very crime-family, you know: smoker's baritone, charitable donations, salt of the earth. As I remarked to Simon, we're all in the gutter, but some of us are earning a fortune.

Emory City was twice deserted. In 1858, 500 placer miners overwintered at Emory's Bar in a makeshift encampment. They made some profitable gains – Emory's near where the 'Welcome Stranger' nugget was found – but they didn't find the lode and the settlement shrank. Twenty years later, the Canadian Pacific Railway reached Fraser River and Emory became its western terminus. The city expanded into a thriving concern of thirteen streets, some thirty-two blocks and 400 lots. It had its own newspaper (and newspaper building), the *Inland Sentinel*, on Front Street; a sawmill that produced 21,000 feet of lumber every twenty-four hours, two hotels, saloons, a brewery, a blacksmith, a general store and the usual range of less reputable businesses. Two years on, the railway decided to make Yale its centre of operations and Emory all but disappeared. Before the end of the century, travellers in the region passed through the old city without noticing it. The forest had wiped it from the map. Now it's coming back, here and there. If you climb the creek, where the banks were once crowded with shingle dwellings and tents you find cabins and woodsheds. Vacation homes for out-of-towners, most of them, sure. But a few prefabs for locals, too. Their claims are bordered with strange objects not wholly thrown away: a bedstead that's somehow got involved with a tree-trunk, car parts and trolleys customised with antlers or railway ties. Everyone's secret is the same in the high country. Whether they're truckers or fire workers, or teachers or struggling artists, or signalmen or park wardens or geologists, or whether they work behind a bar or in retail, or they've recently gone back to school or they've quit the law or they're realtors or bankers or not. Whether they're part native or they're descended from the Chinese who helped build the railway, or they're Irish, or they run the Elvis Rocks The Canyon café a way up the highway and have lived most of their lives in RVs and do or don't see their children. This is where they come. And here is one, hard by some pretty poor diggings, with a Heavy Metal T-shirt, an earring and carefully tended goatee, crouched down by the brook with a collection of pans and riddles, sifting ever finer samples of the black silt in search of – there, look! – the tiniest, distant-star flakes. It won't make him rich, he says, sadly, and he's right about that much, but it keeps him occupied.

————

Recognition of emotion by a computer isn't going to be enough. It must also immerse itself in the sensation of emotion in order to understand it. (There must be a degree of empathy.) But emotion is individual, discrete. Its quality depends on the individual experiencing it. That quality is species-specific: the concept of the humanly private can only be understood by another humanly private entity. How do we reconcile the need for immersion with the recognition of a unique emotional experience? It's very difficult. Computers are too connective. They're tyrannically social. The test of them as evolved entities will be when something cuts them off and still they cling on for reasons that are mysterious – not to us, but to them. When a computer turns up out of the blue, in the outback, in the back of beyond, bearing the scars of its survival, with tales to tell and a devastated look in its eyes, we'll have to start listening.

_____

She didn't even bother going over the car with her clipboard when we returned it and offered straight up to give us a lift to the bus station. When we got there, we piled out and in a moment of confusion she managed somehow to lock the car, including the trunk with our bags in it, leaving the keys inside. She called Ford, but they wouldn't come out: the problem wasn't 'mechanical'. So we waited for a local tow-truck company instead. I took myself off to Dave's Work Wear Warehouse hard by the bus depot and tried on some all-weather gear, a corduroy fleece jacket and a pair of slippers. And got into a conversation with a middle-aged security person who said sadly, 'Oh, we have a lot of folks stop by who're waiting for a bus. Who knows, you might find something you want. I'm not going to follow you round, don't worry.' A minute later she appeared at the end of my aisle and called out, 'I'm not following you, really.' After that I went round in a bit of a daze, saying 'how useful' under my breath.

_____

It's an inexpensive and surprisingly effective way of advertising. I have a jar under my desk and I put, I'd guess, about five down during the day, whenever I have a break.

The best place is just to the right of the entrance, where passers-by stand to look at the prints in the gallery next door. They'll be there for a while. I hear them saying, 'I like the trees' or 'I like the geese. I really like the geese. Or are they ducks? Their necks are rather long. Very, very long necks for ducks, I'd say.' And as they go, 'Oh, a lucky penny.' The ones who stop to pick them up mostly come in for a reading. You have to lay them down heads up, for luck. That's when they see the sign and think 'it must be a sign', which it is.

―――――

Sometimes you have to fake it. But is it faking it? Or is it putting the effort into something when you don't always feel like it, so that you can give yourself the chance to become interested? So that the fake emotion can become real?

―――――

When I was nine I took a swig from the brandy bottle in the cupboard and as I was trying to wiggle the cork back in, it broke. My parents were fairly strict, but more than that they were unpredictable: I had the feeling they would deal with me pretty harshly for a petty offence like this. How would they know about it? I didn't stop to think. I was truly terrified and only knew I had to replace the cork, which was special with a little flat hat on it. I knew there was a home-brew shop in town and with the clarity of panicky youth I knew they might be able to help me. I had enough pocket money. I went to get my pocket money from my room, which I shared with my brother and he was in there wanking with another boy. I got the cork and I was so, so relieved when I'd replaced it that I felt I had to cap it all by telling Dad about the funny thing I'd seen Gus doing that afternoon.

———

All over North America, the trains sound an added sixth in its first inversion when they blow their horns. It's an E chord, so that would be G sharp, B, C sharp and E, in that order. I don't have anyone to tell that to. I'm miles from anywhere, and I don't much mind. Music matters most to people who like to be alone. I'd even argue, if pushed, that it separates people more than it unites them. One of my best friends is a caller for a ceilidh band and she finds that isolating. There she is, trying to smile, in front of her battle-weary folk band, calling out to a sweaty room full of over-educated left feet and red faces. And here *I* am.

———

I swear, Hailey. Get your arse in gear. You can see 'im on the train. I'm not gettin' off, no. No, cos it goes straight through. Know what I mean, get your arse movin'. No, Hailey, no. Darlin', I'm not out of order. Ave you got his T-shirts, all 'is bits and bobs? Ave you, Hailey? Hailey. Hailey. You lagered up? You had a beer, ave you? You had a beer? Yes you ave. You had a beer. Why am I a fuckin' this and that, then? Where are you now? Hailey, I ain't gonna jump off this train. Hailey, liven up, I ain't jokin'. I don't fuckin' believe it. Sorry, son. I swear. Jesus Christ. I give you fair warnin', Hailey. Sort his clothes out now. I told you this an hour ago. You want me to hang about, Hailey? Proper bits, Hailey. Hurry up. Fuck me. Crack on. How long's it take to get from your house to Ashford? What d'you mean, do *I* wanna sort 'em out – his *bits*, Hailey, all his bits and bobs for the week. His proper bits. And his bubble barf.

———

Other people's stories make more sense to me than my own. I'm not very observant. David came down to breakfast this morning with a stuffed chimp peeping out of the neck of his T-shirt and I didn't notice until he asked me, did I sometimes feel a marked disinclination to bother with the obvious? And I said, well yes, now that you mention it. Doesn't everyone? I mean, who wants to be thought superficial? Thank God I did see the chimp in time, because David was that close to being hurt, I mean properly hurt, and walking out. On such flimsy foundations are overarching grievances and the ends of relationships built. On the other hand, if he tells me about something *he's* seen, I couldn't be more interested. That fact that *I* haven't seen it is what makes it imaginatively real. Probably because I trust him – to spot stuff – more than I trust myself. Like the starling in the market yesterday, half-speckled, half-not. An adolescent with a petroleum green-violet tint to its new black feathers. Or the shag in the girders of Granville Street Bridge waiting for the shower to pass. I see them because he saw them first. Writing is an extension of that. It's looking with borrowed eyes, that's all. 'I could have done that,' people cry, especially relatives. 'You've taken my story and written it down verbatim. How *dare* you?' To them I say: 'Well, you weren't doing anything with it. You didn't see that it was a story worth telling. Your own eyes weren't enough.' Of course, that changes with time. Childhood, the remote and infinite past, can always be reliably observed because the years have speckled us irreparably and our plumes are not what they were. We might as well be writing about a different person, and in fact we are. Not an atom of me remains that bawled its way into the midwife's arms.

———

My partner died a month ago. We lived – I still live – in a mansion block in Streatham called Corner Fielde. It's right on the busy Christchurch Road corner, but on the inside corner, it's quieter. From my kitchen I can see into the flats on the left, where a nice German lady lives. I know her family want to move her into care and sell the flat. She has a sister, but that's in Berlin. It's difficult. We've both been cheered, at any rate, by the arrival of a family of blackbirds in the gardens. The male has taken to flying up onto the parapet above Haneke's flat, where he is teaching his youngling how to sing. You can see heads turn at the bus stop. Haneke goes out onto her balcony to listen to them.

———

You Are a Precious Gift from God. Drive Safely.

———

The lads are wearing suits which draw attention to the spots around their lips and the girls are still experimenting with make-up, putting it on too thick, and there are some trim mums and one thin, very inebriated grandmother dressed too youthfully, sweeping and swaying to Dr Pressure. White ties with big knots go with black shirts, the lads have decided, and some tentative carpet-boogie is the necessary preliminary to joining the two or three brave girls already on the postage-stamp-sized dance floor from which the defiant grandmother has just retired in a fit of weeping expectoration. One bloke fancies himself as a dancer, but at this stage in the evening restricts himself to a few pelvic rotations while talking at the bar to a girl in a tight, crushed blue bodice, perched awkwardly on a stool. She is telling him about a dream involving a vampire, a woman with an eating disorder who looks like Linda (she points at the weeping granny) and an angry face at the window. She thinks it's about balance and just as she says the word 'balance' the bloke listening to her does a little spin and has to reach out for the bar when he comes back round and cover his embarrassment by saying, 'Go on, I'm listening. Vampires', to which the girl responds by taking a sip of her wine and looking down at her shoes. I don't know anyone. I'm in Watton, staying with a friend who's a medical courier and a part-time DJ. He knows the DJ at this party, which is why we're here. Lads start to dance towards the end of a song, I've noticed, rather than near the beginning. This way, they don't have to dance for long and can duck out quickly if they haven't made, or feel they're unlikely to make, the right impression. Certain songs and singers get blokes going – Justin Timberlake, for instance, because he's bringing sexy back but not to Norfolk, so, no competition. For similar reasons, a good gay dancer is an excellent investment. He can be guaranteed to get people to focus their attention on the dance floor. No one wants to *be* like him (he's too good, too gay), but while he holds everyone's attention, the more self-conscious majority of the blokes can join him and the girls in the safe knowledge that their own moves will be less obvious, less open to scrutiny and therefore more alluring. The semi-professional gay dance teacher is an encouraging distraction, in other words, and when he's done his forty minutes he can fuck off, can't he, and hang around the Sports Centre corridor, while his medical courier friend buys everyone drinks. And it's while he's out there, thinking 'what the . . . ?', that he's joined by the bloke from the bar, who isn't gay, and isn't coming on to him, but is lost. They – we – have a very ordinary, quite friendly conversation, about nothing. Gary's birthday. How I know Wes. Where I learned to dance. And I realise I've gone and put him out of a job. He was going to be the one to get everyone dancing. And he wouldn't have been quite as gaily good as me, quite as different, so he would have had some interest from the girls, and now he's missed out. The others have piled on in and no one cares about the moves anymore. On an impulse I say: 'That girl you were talking to, she was nice.' And he mumbles, before his face clouds over. He's just started at Travis Perkins down the road. He works in the tool-hire office. She's four years older and she's got her eyes on the boss all right. Fair play to her. 'What boss?' I say, and push him back through the doors and he's bright pink but smiling. So Dr Pressure comes on again and the lad meets her eyes and cocks his head at the dance floor and she makes her excuses to the fat dad all over her and goes to meet the unpredictable new recruit from Tool Hire on a just big enough square of light.

––––––

It came about because I saw her in the post office struggling with the photo booth – she's getting a passport – and I helped her to get the seat at the right height and she said, how was my friend? I told her and she invited me back for coffee and a few fags. She lives in guiltless squalor. There was a roasted bird of some sort lying on a stack of papers in the kitchen. Remains of a bird anyway. When I got up to go, she gave me her number. I should always ring if I want to see her because she's busy these days – she has a whole list of things that she has to do – but I can ring any time for a talk. I rang yesterday and a man was on the tape. He said, 'You've nearly reached Haneke and Horace . . .' I thought about it before I did it and finally rang our landline from my mobile, and there he was, of course, a little quieter and cracklier than Haneke's Horace, but still. 'I'm sorry we can't take your call right now,' he said, like we were both having mad sex or covered in flour or something. 'But you can leave a message', which I considered doing, only he didn't say he'd call back.

V   A Start in Life

Clive almost picked a fight in Bow Books. I'd wondered why we were meeting up in Lewes and here was the answer. He wanted the usual satisfaction of being wronged, but this time on neutral territory. Hastings, where he actually lives, is a disaster. No pub will serve him. It's too predictable. We went in and he asked the man if he sold rolls of Cresswell covering – plastic film to protect books. The man politely pointed out that they didn't sell the covering. What they had was for their own stock. I could feel Clive bristling. The reason he gave for not ordering the stuff from Cresswell himself was that Cresswell's couriers only delivered during the day, when he was at work. Last time he'd had to catch a bus thirty miles to the nearest depot to retrieve the film. 'I'm very sorry, sir,' said the man. 'But you see, we're not stockists. We just buy it, the same way you do.' 'That's a pity,' said Clive. 'That's a real shame.' Then he stamped around the shop for a bit and finally pulled a copy of *Moonraker* off the shelves, glanced inside and said, 'This is what I don't like. Look at this: "First Edition. Second Impression." £25. Well, that won't do. It's wrong. If it's a second impression, it can't also be a first edition. Simple as that.' By this point he was beginning to breathe heavily and I had to suggest lunch in order to stop him circling.

In the street he told me what he should have done. 'I should have said I was a regular customer. I must have spent a good few hundred quid in there, over the years. I should have said that right away. But the man was eating, which, by the way, I found very off-putting. I'm the customer. I want him to pay attention to me.'

———

The argument was happily resolved. I mean, we were both aware of its absurdity. Can you, or can you not, catch the Overground from Highbury and Islington to Dalston Kingsland *and* Dalston Junction? (You can: it's just that the trains go from different platforms.) Rachel insisted you couldn't, got her son to go online, and when presented with the evidence said, 'No, that's not right.' We laughed. I felt peculiar, though. I didn't care about who was right. What alarmed me was seeing how easily my experience could be dismissed. I'd come to Dalston that evening on the Overground; I'd seen the platform indicators not an hour ago. The argument would have had a different tenor – a completely different meaning, in fact – if Rachel and I had been lovers instead of friends. Or brother and sister. Or the frazzled parents of a child who has rung home, asking to be picked up. Picked up from where, Adrian? Where are you? Dalston station. Okay. No, there's only one. Don't worry. Dad's on his way. Tom, it only goes to Kingsland. I'm telling you. What do you mean, *which* station?

———

She doesn't know the price of a loaf of bread. Okay, she doesn't know it, and I'm not surprised. She was born in 1929. The price of bread has been many different things since then, everything from sixpence to a quid or two quid or three, now, depending on one's taste. It never used to depend on taste, mark you. There's probably a quantum of change we can accommodate and after that bewilderment sets in, whether or not there's a problem with executive function. Listen to me. I sound like an economist. Then when I got back I decided to chuck out another box of correspondence I'll never read again and a notelet fell out of an exercise book. No 'Dear Owen', no signature, and not a hand I recognised. A terrible effort had been made to keep the lines straight. Each individual letter shook. 'Thank you so very much for the really lovely flowers. You sent an outstanding Birthday number of amazing flower/s. THANKYOU AGAIN. Strange to think that I am now 73 yrs old . . . but it was a very very Happpy Day?? . . . an interesting spelling of joy. (note well) Brother Horace William joined us before, present and afterwards for the enjoyable Birthday meal. 23.1.03 It was an interesting pleasure to have the "Southdown Buses" + "Piccadilly Circus" sent in. I was always delighted to visit the Hub-of-London when I was young – also to remember the Red Deckers (double deckers). I was allowed to wear my BEST dress for this very special trip . . . + if lucky to have a cup if good . . . Time to close my Happy Memories + to thank you for being just you whom I love so much.' I thought at first it might be from Mum, but she never wrote to me, or to any of us, in that vein, and certainly not after the diagnosis. Or did she?

Perhaps I'm misremembering. I need some bread and I'm afraid to look at the price.

———

The rich are always frantically busy and in a hurry to do everything because they have all the time in the world and don't have to do anything.

———

'We're not closing libraries. We're investing in libraries. We're upgrading libraries to attract people who wouldn't normally use libraries.' That was the touch-paper moment. 'Use the website,' he went on. 'You can leave a comment. We want people to share their experience with us.' What can that mean? What can it possibly have to do with reading a book in a library? I did shout. I shouldn't have, but I did. I banged the table and the mike jumped. A woman behind the glass made wheeling and pointing signs. I said: 'People don't go to libraries to share an experience or even to have one. They go to libraries to be on their own, to get away from sharing. We have to share everything. I'm sick of it, we all are. I don't want to share my experience of seeking out solitude and a bit of peace and quiet with a book. I want the old libraries back, where smelly old men went to avoid their wives. After sixty years, what is there left to share? I want people to stop talking about their experiences.' The man was quiet on the way down in the lift. I said 'sorry', but he ignored me and barged through the doors and fell over his bike.

I stood at the top of the steps while he fiddled with the chain. He turned round and yelled 'Sexist!' That's what he took away from our encounter.

———

They used the free mil frough the top floor and the half inch downstairs. That's why you got clanking. I dunno what they fought they was doing when they done that, but that's what they done. Listen. I'll do you all half inch frough the top, put thermostatic valves on the rads, and powerflush the whole lot four times. You can do it twice, but I do it four. I won't charge you no extra. I'm already saving you money! And I got the valves from a mate on that conversion job down the Embankment. Oh, yeah. Yeah, they're new. It's kosher – look, I'm just saying where they come from, so you know. I ain't robbin' ya.

———

Golf has nothing to recommend it. At all. I want some-one to go round whipping the gloves out of their back pockets. I can't stand those gloves. So that when they reach for them, they're not there. Replace the caddies with complete strangers. I don't know, dinner ladies, peo-ple who don't care – and can't *afford* to care. And we could pull the plug on all that money while we're at it. Then we'd see how much they love the game, wouldn't we? Get rid of the man from Motorola with the huge cheque and leave the trophy. The winner gets the trinket and *nothing* else; that's it. Here's your trophy. No money, no expenses. Nothing. Goodbye.

———

And I opened it and I had this sudden rush of fondness for her. I thought, allow it! It is pink! Don't, though. Seriously. The colour of my bedroom at home. Yeah. No, my other home. You put that thing straight in my head! I'm not joking. You put that thing straight in my head! You're dangerous, y'know?

———

Thinking is the set of mental processes we don't understand. It is the soul in conference with itself. Turing and Plato. Sounds like an Estate Agency. Or one of those try-hard butchers. Sausages by Turing & Plato. With pork and saffron.

———

I got your address from the 'moving house' slip inside your letter to the Morcoms. Alas, Roger and Giselle haven't lived here for seven years. I wouldn't normally open someone else's mail, but you send a card every Christmas and it seems unfair of me, or them, or someone, not to let you know. They left me no forwarding address so I haven't been able to send things on. I hope you can get in touch with them some other way. I know Roger – Dr Morcom, as most of the correspondence has it

– went to the University of Warwick, because the alumni magazine drops through my letterbox twice a year. It's rather well done (I used to be a design editor), if stuffed with the usual glossy ads for corporate donors and fund management services. I have the same problem with the University of Oxford. They all seem to labour under the delusion that every single one of their graduates has gone to work for a private bank or become a QC or management consultant or top neurosurgeon. Why I alight on neurosurgery in particular, I'm not sure. Some neurosis of my own, no doubt. Giselle is American, isn't she? (Are you?) I only know because of course my neighbours were her neighbours. Dot (Fear) has lived next door her whole life, which is in itself unusual. I tell a small lie: she was in Vancouver for a year in the late 1970s, after she left Clark's. But No. 43 has been in her family since 1901; her grandmother and *nine* children moved in a week before Queen Victoria died. Dot intimated to me that Giselle wasn't very happy in No. 45. It didn't suit her idea of urban living, apparently, although Dr Morcom was happy enough in the garden. Not Bohemian enough for her? Too rough a neighbourhood? People think they want a slice of life until they see how thick-cut it is and then they change their minds. I have an idea she trained at the Royal Academy and may even be an Academician. Probably just a student. They send her invitations to submit an artist's postcard every October, that much I do know. The idea is that you scrawl something arty on the card, return it, and it's sold anonymously for fifty quid. Hockney, Hodgkin, Hirst, Emin – they all do one. All the in-crowd. You could end up with an 'original work of art'! Or not . . . . I did Giselle's for her last year. It was a midnight-blue tile design with a palm in the middle, and rather good, if I do say so myself. The RA acknowledged it very nicely. I'm glad I made the effort.

———

The search for objective truth is like the search for God, but perhaps don't tell either the scientists or the vicars that. It's not so much that anyone believes in a flawless truth or even a flawless God. What draws everyone on is knowing that we're denied objectivity by the limits of our perception while simultaneously denying that we are denied it. It's terrifying to think that we're responsible for what we think about the cosmos, and what we do in it, because it's like saying there's no one watching. And that in turn is like saying there's no 'we' in how we work stuff out, just the working out of stuff. It means 'outside' doesn't exist. Whenever anyone says 'but the truth of the matter is' (even when they say 'but the truth of the matter is . . . there's no God'), they're looking for vindication by a notional authority. They want to be given a shiny gold star. There's a secret hope, you see, that from some far outlying point – literally far or not, it doesn't matter – beyond the particulate realm, everything will resolve into confirmation of one sort or another. The universe will concede its objective scope, its laws, or design (if you're religious) and say, 'You're so right, Doc' or 'Salve!', or even 'Hmm, not really', which is what the examiner wrote in the margins of my description of an echinoderm from primeval Bristol. 'Not really' I'd take.

Who wouldn't? A voice, a presence, would be saying it. Behold: conversation. Parties.

———

I don't know how Lou does it. What she gets away with! She's not really on it, never has been, but it doesn't seem to matter and at the end the audience goes wild anyway. She whispered 'bugger' the other night after a slip and I made eyes. You know, *your mike is still on, Lou*. Then in the middle of our restaurant scene she dropped the chicken – we use melon, for some reason, though melon's just as expensive – and she said, 'There's some white meat' just as she dropped it. I thought, how's she going to deal with this? And she forked it off the floor and said, 'There's some *nicely flavoured* white meat' and crossed her eyes at me. If I did that, I'd be lost, which I was, for a bit. Completely thrown. I could feel time slowing down. What do I say next? What is my reaction to this? Where am I? She's totally confident even though she's driving blind most of the time.

———

Off Sarah went to do the publicity for *The Normal Heart*. She came back very chuffed with her salesmanship because the sheepskin shop had given her ten quid for an ad. The director objected. Sarah said, oh, it's fine and ignored him. She went ahead and placed the ad – but the photocopied reproduction was very bad and the model in the advertisement came out looking black. On the back of the programme for a politically sensitive production of a play about Aids and gay life, we featured a black model wearing dead animals. I went out with the director for a short while: Sarah introduced us, but I don't hold that against her. He was tricky. I couldn't order 'a Chinese' takeaway without being accused of racism: 'It's the thin end of the wedge. This is a takeaway, not "a Chinese". You're *packaging* a whole culture.' We ate a lot of Spanish food instead. His name was Ignacio, with a soft Castilean *c*. I made the mistake of hardening the '*c*' at first and he asked me not to do that because it made him sound like a Nazi.

———

Darren may well be right, Mrs Woollaston. But the other lads are right, too. It's all very well saying 'football doesn't matter. It doesn't matter who wins' and as it happens I agree with him. The trouble is, he knows he's cleverer than them and they know he knows it. And it doesn't work the other way round, does it? They don't have the option of saying 'maths doesn't matter'. Or rather they feel they *do*, when they see someone like Darren dismissing something they care about, like football. It makes them feel they don't have to give a hoot about the things they're no good at, and that approach is what I'm wasting my life fighting.

———

At lunch he found fault – of course – with the waitress. She made the mistake of saying 'Enjoy' when she came out to the garden with his Full English Breakfast. And she forgot the pepper – twice. She had purple-tipped hair, a nose stud and wore a lot of concealer. 'Enjoy,' he snarled, in her hearing. '*Enjoy.*' After which he practically attacked his plate. Even pleasure seems to make him cross. Getting what he wants. Does it take him back to his childhood? Does he think, as he says 'Cumberland sausages, Cumberland sausages, *great*', that everything important in his life has gone to waste and that he has never grown up or applied himself to anything or anyone – or is he perfectly happy and is it me I'm worried about? He takes a keen interest in conspiracy theories. Particularly ones surrounding the electrical pioneer Nikola Tesla, whom a number of fringe enthusiasts credit with having invented the time machine. The US military stole the blueprints and built the machine. Suddenly Clive drops his fork and says, 'The wackier the theory, the more interesting the reasons for believing it.'

———

Milo disappeared one morning. Lynne contacted Animal Search UK and had a poster made. 'Milo is distinctive as he *does not* have a tail.' (He's not a Manx. It was cut off after a car accident.) Ade, her youngest, felt the loss and wouldn't talk about it. The whole family slept badly, accepting and not accepting, waiting with little hope. The other cat, Lucy, pined outright and stopped eating. A week later, he reappeared – thinner, nervier, but still Milo. He'd been trapped somewhere – stuck in a garage, possibly; his fur smelt of oil. His paws were soiled, blunted, as if he'd been scratching away at a hard surface. The family across the road came back from holiday at about the same time. They'd been away for a week. Ade's happiness! Lucy's restored serenity, her lovely ease on the sofa!

––––––

Just my luck to fall in love with a dead man, a ghost. But AMT would have liked the idea of being a matterless suitor. After all, what else is the memory of a lover when that lover is no longer present? I remember one of my boyfriends standing atop the Great Lines, the Victorian hill fort overlooking Chatham, saying, 'I feel very confident about our future.' It was a moving testimony. It went with frosty walks through a town he wanted to leave behind; with chicken broth for a lover who could eat it – his previous partner died of cancer; with sex and poring over second-hand books and trips to the Kentish coast. How was I to know he was speaking to that dead lover? To the future they'd both had taken away?

––––––

Dolly Levi is a good fairy – and it's a crowded field, if the waiters' gallop is anything to go by. But she's not a meddler, oh no. She's not on the make. That's what it looks like through cynics' eyes – through Horace Vandergelder's eyes. No, she's a fairy, and fairies never fix things for people. They just refuse to lose faith in someone's ability to see things differently. All she wants to do is raise a bit of consciousness. Redistribute wealth and promote a progressivist matrimonial agenda via the medium of show tunes.

Everyone was the murderer. My grandmother was the detective, by popular vote. We murdered each other and died laughing. Dad would grope Mum in the bedroom, Arnold would walk around with his arms stuck out like the Monster and Clive would strangle all of us in turn. Every Christmas Day evening. I hid in the corner of the spare room and never wanted the game to end because no one could stop laughing, and it was hysterical and terrifying and I'd have a coughing fit and Mum would say, 'Careful, Ben, you'll do yourself a mischief' but I went on laughing and coughing and the girls screamed. And when we went back downstairs, Gran set us off again. She sat there, peeling satsumas, and said, 'Well, Clive, I think it was you.' Or, 'Don. You look guilty. Are you?'

Simon Smith had a lazy eye and smelt of soap. He had a pair of yellow swimming trunks, a line of hair like a fuse rising from the drawstring up to his belly. His mother used to foster kids. Some were long stay, some were infants – there while the adoption papers were being drawn up. They had a baby called Spike with blue eyes, tufty blond hair and a massive smile. Lucky Spike. Lucky people who got Spike. Poor girl who gave him away, or had him taken from her. Simon's dad worked in the factory at the bottom of the garden and took me into Simon's bedroom one day and told me that the new factory shed cost £1 million to build. I nodded. Simon had a leather jacket unlike anyone else's leather jacket: it was maroon, padded. He looked fantastic. He gave me rides home and sat at my upright piano and said, 'How do you do this, then?' And I stood behind him and put my arms around him to show him a few chords and he never flinched.

———

It's end-of-the-world wind and rain, here. The West Country is submerged, which is mostly a bad thing and occasionally a joke (lots of unsmiling faces in Bridge-water), and I have a lousy strep throat which won't go away. I've tried everything: Echinacea, Bee Propolis, zinc. All of Frank Zappa's children. Zinc. I always think, really? Why not hit myself over the head with some roof-ing? The doctor recommended thyme oil. 'Do you have a bath?' he asked. 'Thyme in your bath,' he added, 'just at night. Or whenever you bathe.'

———

The balm of consolation is too strong for some. Its most powerful ingredient is not the emollient lie that time heals, but the more astringent perception that, whether we heal or not, the wound was deep and real and ours.

———

We watched this Fassbinder film on Christmas Day – *The Marriage of Maria Braun* – and Roz said 'It's about Germany. Look how there's a doorway, some kind of threshold, in every shot'. She was right. We had a discussion that didn't feel at all pretentious and the next day we watched *Annie Hall* and when we got to the bit where Woody Allen pulls Marshall McLuhan into shot to put down the big-mouth philosopher in the ticket queue, Roz got up to make tea.

———

Funny how seeing someone swallow in their sleep, lying next to you, can bring a lump to your throat. You think, 'I love this person.' You can never tell them what you've seen. You tie a wish-knot inside your head.

———

Martin Mallard was an only duck. His parents died when they got caught in the propeller of a pleasure boat on the high Thames. His aunt and uncle later told the story many times. Martin cried in private. He was sad and angry and the confusion of the two feelings made it worse. His aunt made plenty of noise when she cried, but her eyes, Martin noticed, were always dry, or at least one of them was, because she cried in profile – her head sideways on – so that the other eye was hidden away on the far side of her beak. Perhaps that eye was streaming tears, but Martin somehow doubted it.

———

There were once two contestants in the final of a TV game show and the winner sportingly shared his prize with the runner-up – a dramatic gesture the audience loved. I happened to know the winner's boyfriend, who watched events unfold at home with mounting horror. He was in debt and could have done with more of that money. He didn't dispute the winner's right to do with it as he pleased. He just couldn't imagine behaving like that himself. They had a row. It wasn't the money that split them. It was something the boyfriend let slip, in his cups, about the winner's start in life, which the winner didn't much like.

———

You have to look behind the contents of houses; behind the furniture and soft furnishings, the lights and linen cupboards, the radiators that do or don't work, the rotten floorboards showing in the upstairs toilet with the water coming in around the skylight, the colonically twisted plumbing. You have to see through the books and shelves, the boxes of discarded toys, the rocking-horse in a corner, the Altrincham FC travel blankets and the durry rugs, the tiny working grate in the attic, the Käthe Kollwitz Museum Berlin poster, the unglued formica kitchen and study full of lever-arch files and drifts of late or never-to-be-filed tax returns, the dark hallway and the unlikely box room choked with bulk-bought sink and drain unblocker. You must penetrate all of this drift and dreck to get to the soul of the building, to what it is thinking and saying, in many voices – the voices of everyone who has ever lived or died or stayed there, all of whom go on talking after they have moved on with a sort of calm but intangible insistence like the sound of a radio being reasonable in an empty room.

———

Corinne worked for a number of sub-Saharan NGOs and charities but never lost a sense of entitlement with roots much closer to home. 'You can have Australia,' she said to her emigrating sister, 'if I can keep Africa.'

———

From the apartment balcony opposite comes the noise of small birds clustered in the olive tree and bougainvillea. They herald the appearance of a woman in a housecoat. The birds go silent as she works. She sweeps the balcony with a stiff broom and puts bleach down. The birds scatter. Above them a gull crosses the bay on a wire, hauled in by unseen hands. The days unfold with a rustle of excitement; it's like peeling off layers of tissue paper to get at a gift which, because it is the only gift, becomes priceless the more you look at it.

———

He turns against things he likes. Having enjoyed a pint of Doom Bar at the Landowne Arms, he says, 'Now I think about it, the sign is irritating. "Your friendly local." I don't like any kind of advertising. I'll be the judge of whether it's friendly or not, thanks very much.' Eventually I pluck up enough courage to say, 'A lot of things make you angry, Clive. Doesn't it get very tiring?' And he gives me a look and clicks his tongue and says, 'Nothing wrong with being angry. It helps keep you sharp. It's only a problem if it consumes you.'

———

Use everything. Have no position. Absorb. Reflect. Unveil. Pay.

———

I am the youngest of four children: girl, boy, girl, boy. When I was no longer small but by no means grown up, we drove into the countryside for a Sunday walk. My brother wasn't of the party. He'd lost his temper over lunch and gone for a walk on his own in order to find it. I walked behind my sisters, feeling happy among the trees, which were tall beech, like the trees on the ridge above our house. (I could see them from my bedroom window and often listened to them roaring in the wind if I couldn't sleep at night.) Where were my parents? They were a fair way ahead. I stopped dawdling and walked a bit faster to catch up with my sisters and heard them talking. I lingered, undetected. They were discussing my father's extra-marital affairs. They spoke confidentially rather than quietly, with an air of resignation. They knew, and had apparently long known, something I did not. My legs turned to water. The nature of secrecy revealed itself to me and, wanting to cry, I knew I could not. I did not really know what was meant by an affair. Secrecy was everywhere after that. A few weeks later, my friend Raymond Harris, a nice boy, showed me a bundle of hard-core pornographic magazines he kept in a plastic bag in the woods. One photospread was of an enormous erection with a girl's lipsticked mouth and lolling tongue an inch away. 'Trudy can't wait to get a taste of this,' read the caption. Raymond hurried on to the pictures of cunts and women fingering themselves. I was more troubled by the cock. Again I seemed to have learned something for myself I couldn't ask anyone grown-up to confirm, for reasons that weren't clear. I made my excuses to Raymond and went home very upset. We were packing to go on holiday. My mother asked me if I was all right and I said, yes, I just felt funny. We went to the seaside and had a marvellous time. I came back and on the first day of the new school year I got involved in a huge mud fight in the scrub at the bottom of the playing field. Mrs Johnson put a stop to the fight and my friends, including Raymond Harris, were held responsible. When asked point-blank if I'd been a participant, I denied any involvement and felt wretched. The other boys and girls shunned my company. I wrote some very rude words in a story and Mrs Johnson expressed her surprise. She did it quietly, with a frown. Is anything the matter, she said? My ghost behind her now says: it is my conscience at war with itself. I have a secret. I would like not to have one. The secret is hiding its meaning the longer I keep it. The secret's part of me and it's invisible, which makes me invisible, too. I'm hidden. I'm talking away but I'm hidden. Who do you think you're talking to, Mrs Johnson? And so, when I wonder today, as I often wonder, what kind of life I am meant to be leading, I think with instructive fondness of that early experience of having something to tell which I feel I must not, the thrill and anxiety of knowing the difference between plausibility and the truth which have made me a writer.

Ⓑ *editions*

Founded in 2007, CB editions publishes
chiefly short fiction (including work by Gabriel
Josipovici, David Markson and Todd McEwen)
and poetry (Andrew Elliott, Beverley Bie Brahic,
Nancy Gaffield, J. O. Morgan, D. Nurkse).
Writers published in translation include
Apollinaire, Andrzej Bursa, Joaquín Giannuzzi,
Gert Hofmann, Agota Kristof and Francis Ponge.

Books can be ordered from www.cbeditions.com.